The Quarterback Sneak

THE QUARTERBACK SNEAK

Randy Petersen

Tyndale House Publishers, Inc.
Wheaton, Illinois

Books in the Choice Adventures series

1 *The Mysterious Old Church*

2 *The Smithsonian Connection*

3 *The Underground Railroad*

4 *The Rain Forest Mystery*

5 *The Quarterback Sneak*

6 *The Monumental Discovery*

7 *The Abandoned Gold Mine*

8 *The Hazardous Homestead*

Cover illustration copyright © 1992 by John Walker
Copyright © 1992 by The Livingstone Corporation

Library of Congress Cataloging-in-Publication Data

Petersen, Randy
  The quarterback sneak / Randy Petersen.
    p. cm. — (Choice adventures ; #5)
  Summary: The reader's choices control the adventures that six
friends have involving tickets to a Washington Redskins game and a
homeless family.
  ISBN 0-8423-5029-2
  1. Plot-your-own stories. [1. Plot-your-own stories.
2. Adventure and adventurers—Fiction. 3. Homeless persons—Fiction.
4. Christian life—Fiction.] I. Title. II. Series.
PZ7.P44199Qu   1992
[Fic]—dc20   91-38124

Printed in the United States of America

99 98 97 96 95 94 93 92
 9   8   7   6   5   4   3   2   1

"**G**o out for a pass." Chris Martin had two cans of soda pop in his hands. He was nudging his pal Willy.

In a flash, Willy was speeding down the sidewalk. Joining the fun, Pete reached out with his long arms and tried to "sack" Chris. Sam blocked him.

Twenty yards away, Willy faked left and turned right. Chris dodged behind a lamppost for some extra blocking and hurled one of the pop cans in a perfect spiral, right into Willy's waiting hands.

"Touchdown!" the four boys yelled, raising their arms high. Without thinking, Willy spiked the can into the sidewalk. It erupted in a foamy mess.

Willy looked sadly at the exploded can. "That was my last fifty cents," he moaned. "And I was really thirsty, too."

"No problem, big guy," said Chris, fishing some money out of his pocket. "I'm loaded. Let me treat you." They all headed back to High's, the store they had just left.

High's was a short brick building on one of the main streets of Millersburg. It didn't have much, but it had soda pop, candy, and baseball cards. The Ringers often stopped there on their way home from school. Now that it was summertime, they only went there when they had nothing else to do.

This was one of those days. The weather was hot and muggy. All afternoon the four of them had been saying,

2

"What do you wanna do?" "Nothing. What do you wanna do?" "I don't know." Finally one of them said, "Hey, let's go down to High's." Willy's spiking of the can was the most excitement they had seen all day.

The store had a sign on its door that said Only Two Kids Permitted at One Time. So Sam and Pete stayed outside.

"I hate that sign," Pete muttered.

"Yeah, me too," said Sam as they waited. "You know, someday I'm going to start a store, and I'm going to put up a sign that says Only Two Adults Permitted at One Time."

Before long, the other two came out. Willy was carefully sipping a Mountain Dew. Sam playfully bumped him—"Don't spill!" Willy gave him a dirty look, then smiled.

"Look what I got," crowed Chris, unwrapping a small package in his hands. "Football cards!"

"Already?" said Willy.

"They must have just gotten them in," Chris answered. "It's a good thing we went back. I didn't see them before."

"Who do you have?" The boys were crowding around Chris. They had all traded baseball cards since they were little. It was only last year that they started with football cards. (One year they even tried hockey cards, but it didn't catch on.)

Chris was examining each card and handing it to Willy, who checked it and passed it on to Pete, who glanced at it before handing it to Sam, who simply put it in his back pocket. Sam was the least interested in football cards. Suddenly Chris stopped. "Look at this! Reggie Sanders!"

"Oh, man! He is awesome!" Willy howled.

"He's going to take the Redskins all the way this year," Chris added.

"You know," Willy said, grinning back at Chris, "you looked like another Reggie Sanders yourself when you threw that soda can."

Chris's face lit up. "You really think so? I mean, he's my idol."

"Do not worship idols," Sam piped up. "Wasn't that what we learned in Sunday school last week?"

Willy flipped a card at him, which Sam deftly caught and looked at. "Deacon Joe Johnson," he read. "Who's he?"

"Not much," Chris grunted, still looking at Reggie Sanders's statistics. "Deacon Joe's a lineman for the Redskins. He's pretty much washed up."

"He's got a card full of numbers," Sam continued. "Is that good?"

"He *was* good," said Willy. He hated it when Sam tried to make a point. "He's just not doing much anymore."

"They think this is his last year," Chris added, *"if* he makes the team."

"Hmmm," was all Sam could say. He was deep in thought.

The boys finished their drinks and put the cans in the recycling bin in back of the store. "Hey, what happened to the cards?" Chris asked.

They all shook their heads. Chris retraced his steps from the door of the store. The other three fanned out, searching the ground carefully. Suddenly Sam stopped.

4

CHOICE ⇒

Turn to page 34.

Chris was definitely interested in what Betty's surprise was, but he couldn't imagine leaving his friend right now. Willy really needed him. They had been fast friends since fourth grade, and there were many times when Willy had been there for him.

The others said their good-byes, with a promise to report back later. Then they trooped over to the Freeze.

On the way they talked some about Willy's injury, but soon their thoughts turned to ice cream and surprises.

"Hi, Betty!" they called as they filed into the Freeze and found four counter stools to sit (and spin) on. "Got any surprises for us?"

"Do I ever!" said Betty, as she finished ringing up a customer's order. "But first you have to answer my riddle. Eleven members of a football team took a test. They all failed it, except one. Who was it?"

Betty hurried off to clean a table as the kids pondered her riddle.

"Eleven football players took the test," Pete repeated.

"And all but one failed," added Jill.

"Sounds like the University of Virginia," Sam quipped. No one laughed. They were deep in thought.

"Let's think this through," said Jill. "Say we're all on a football team. We take a test. I fail. Sam fails. Pete fails."

"And I pass," said Tina.

6

A smile slowly crossed Pete's face. "That's it. I know the answer."

Turn to page 99.

Sam decided to wait fifteen more seconds for Pete to come back. Then, if anything happened to him, it would be Pete's fault for being so slow.

Five, six, seven . . . There was that voice again, high and fast, almost like a person talking in an excited way. *Ten, eleven* . . . By now Sam was hoping Pete wouldn't come back. He wanted to check out that voice. *Fourteen, fifteen*.

Time's up.

Ten feet into the tunnel, Sam thought he should have given Pete another fifteen seconds. It was creepy down there. Sam held his arms out in front of him and walked slowly, but still, every so often, a root would scratch his head or poke his side. Then the tunnel got narrower. Sam had to get down on all fours to continue.

Just for a moment, he saw a dot of light in the circle of the tunnel ahead of him. It looked like a match and a hand holding it. But who—or what—was attached to that hand?

Maybe I should go back, he thought. *I've seen enough. Pete's probably there by now to rescue me. We can come back here sometime with flashlights.*

He tried to crawl backwards through the narrow space. It was slow going. Finally, he got to the place where the tunnel was larger. He stood up, stretched his cramped legs, and turned around.

8

Suddenly, in the darkness, he felt something slide against him. It came from the tunnel behind him—where he had just been—brushed his legs and moved in front of him. He gasped with surprise, and he heard a high-pitched squeak. Just then, there was the crisp sound and sharp smell of a match lighting, and for a moment there was a burst of firelight in front of him.

He saw a face. It was small and ratlike. It seemed to have human features, but the skin was brown and gray. Sam screamed. The creature screamed. The sound filled the tunnel, and the match went out. There was only darkness now and a deafening wall of sound.

Sam turned to run. Hitting his head against the narrowing tunnel, he dropped to his knees and crawled as quickly as he could to get away from the awful beast. He knew he was moving away from the hole in the ground, where Pete was probably looking for him by now. But he had to hurry, before the giant rodent could catch him. The tunnel bent slightly, and he saw a light in the distance.

As he drew closer, he saw that it was a candle. The tunnel opened into a slightly wider area. To Sam's right, the tunnel continued; to the left was a small alcove. The stubby candle burned in one corner. Sam was amazed to see a collection of odd objects: a can of Mountain Dew, a length of rope, a beat-up suitcase, some newspapers, a McDonald's bag with something in it, a bottle of ketchup, and four tickets to a Redskins game.

He heard a sound behind him. The creature was probably coming after him. He whirled around and saw a dim shape moving toward him. He looked over at where the tunnel continued on. Should he try to escape? Or should he stay and confront the creature where he could see it?

He had only a moment to decide.

CHOICE

If Sam stays to confront the creature, turn to page 81.

If Sam escapes through the tunnel, turn to page 40.

10

Tina's statement made Jill stop and think. Jill had never had Tina's great-aunt—known to most of the Ringers as Miss Whitehead—as a Sunday school teacher. But she had heard a lot about her. She noticed how quiet the boys got whenever Miss Whitehead's name came up. *She must have been a really special lady,* Jill thought. She knew the boys felt they'd learned a lot from Miss Whitehead. And she knew they missed her.

OK, so if Miss Whitehead taught them so much, Jill thought, *why are they still so ornery?* Why didn't the *boys* start the niceness? Why didn't Miss Whitehead teach them to treat girls as real people and not like somebody's day-old lunch bag? Maybe she had taught them that and they just forgot.

In any case, those boys needed to learn a lesson. This was a great opportunity to teach them one. Jill told Tina about her plan, and Tina reluctantly agreed. Then Jill swaggered over to explain it to the boys.

"It's simple. We'll take the next three days to decide who goes with us. Whoever is nicest to us in those three days gets the tickets. Got it? You be nice to us, and we'll be nice to you. We'll make our final decision on Friday."

Sam slammed his glass of water down on the table. "I don't like it," he muttered. In a moment, he was up and headed toward the door.

"What's wrong?" Pete called after him.

Sam turned to face the others, his hand on the door. "I'm going to be nice to you because I like to be nice to you and because it's right—not because of some stupid tickets. I don't like this at all. It's like you're playing God."

Then the door jangled and he was gone. The mother and daughter in the other booth looked up from their sundaes to see what was wrong. The little boy, who was twirling on a counter stool, stopped in midtwirl. The boyfriend and girlfriend in the back didn't pay any attention. All the Ringers just stared in disbelief. Sam didn't talk a whole lot. But when he said something, it was either funny or smart. This wasn't very funny.

The door jangled again. Suddenly Sam was standing there, as if he'd never left. "And another thing," he continued. "I said you were playing God, but you're not. Because God doesn't say, 'You be nice to me and I'll be nice to you.' He's good to us all the time, whether we treat him right or not. So I was wrong. You're not playing God. I don't know what you're playing, but it's not God."

With another jangle, he was gone again.

Pete unfolded his lanky frame, sliding from the booth. "I'm going after Sam," he said under his breath. He took a few swift strides to the door, then turned and said, "I think he's right."

Jangle.

Turn to page 52.

12

"It's the one where Jesus said, 'Where two or three are gathered together in my name, I am there with them.'"

Sam laughed.

"You said you wouldn't laugh!" Pete said, feeling a little hurt.

"I'm not laughing *at* you," Sam explained. "I just think it's funny. Jesus—here in the pit with us. I never thought of that before. I mean, where would he fit?"

"And how could he help us get out of here?"

"Yeah," Sam agreed, and he was suddenly serious. "What would he want us to do?"

"Apologize," Pete said softly.

Sam knew it was true. "Yeah," he said, "I'm sorry for yelling at you just now."

"Me too," said Pete. "You're my best friend, Sam."

"You too. And even though I make fun of you sometimes, you know I'm just joking. You're a real good guy. No kidding."

"You, too, Sam. I mean, like, what you said back at the Freeze about playing God and everything. That was hard to say. But I think you were right. And I told the others that. So I just want you to know that I support and stand behind you."

"Thanks, Pete. Just knowing that, well, it really gives

me a lift. I mean—uh . . . " Sam stopped short. "Wait a minute . . . what did you just say, Pete?"

"Uh, I really support you, and I stand behind you."

"And what did I say?"

"It really gives you a lift."

"That's our answer, Pete! Maybe Jesus really *is* here with us!" If there had been any room in the hole, Sam would have been jumping around in excitement. As it was, he had to squeeze around Pete to show him what he meant. "Here, put your hands like this and let me step up."

In a few moments, Sam was standing on Pete's shoulders and hauling himself up out of the pit. Once out, he ran to the Freeze to get some rope. Fortunately, Betty had a strong one in the basement. Sam tied one end to a tree and dropped the other into the pit. Pete climbed out easily.

They called the county office and reported the hole. A construction crew filled it in later that day.

The Ringers came up with all sorts of theories about why the hole was there. Some said it was where the local militia hid its weapons during the Revolutionary War. Others said it had to do with the Underground Railroad and hiding runaway slaves. Still others thought it was dug by the Secret Service as an observation post when President Eisenhower visited the town in 1956.

However it got there, all Sam and Pete knew was that their friendship was stronger thanks to those few minutes in "the pit." Though the others thought they were a little nuts, they were actually glad they had fallen into it.

14

CHOICE ⇒

Haven't met Greg and his girlfriend yet? How about Reggie Sanders? If not, turn to page 34 and try other options.

Over the next few days, Jill was troubled. The doctor had told Willy he couldn't go to the game because of his crutches. But she kept thinking about how much Chris would like going to the game. It was just that she wanted to go, too.

The Tuesday before the game, just after dinner, Jill said, "Chris, I have something to give you."

She held her hands behind her back to increase his suspense. "I know we had a fight last week about girls playing football, and I hope I proved something to you in that game at Willy and Chris's apartment. But you proved something to me, too. You could have left Willy and gone to the Freeze with us, but you're a good friend to Willy, and so you stayed with him. That's what good friends do. And I don't think you should be left out because of it. So here, enjoy the game."

She held out the ticket to him. Chris took it in surprise. "But what about you?"

"You'll have more fun than I would." She smiled. "Go on, take it."

"Thanks, Jill. You know, you're a pretty good friend yourself."

For a moment, he wanted to hug her, but he couldn't get himself to move.

16

The next day, Tina asked Jill, "So what are you going to wear to this game?"

"Nothing."

Tina looked shocked. "Really, you'd better wear *something*. There'll be boys there."

"No, I mean I'm not going. I gave my ticket to Chris."

"So now I'll be the only girl with three boys."

"That's not so bad, Tina."

"Come on, Jill. We're talking about Sam, Pete, and Chris!"

"Yeah, you're right."

"I mean, they'll be talking about touchdowns and wide receivers and Richie Simmons—"

"Sanders," Jill corrected. "Reggie Sanders."

"See? What do I know? Where I come from, the footballs are round, and you're not allowed to touch them with your hands."

"You mean soccer?"

"They call it 'football' in Brazil."

Tina went home, thinking hard. Finally she decided to offer her ticket to Willy. But Willy would not be recovered in time for the game, so Tina was going to offer it to Jill. But then Tina's brother, Jim, came back from camp for the weekend. So Chris gave his ticket to Jim, saying that he'd rather watch the game on TV with Willy—and Jill. Then, since her brother was going, Tina figured it wouldn't be so bad to go with the others—even if they were all boys.

So that's how it worked out. Pete, Sam, Tina, and Jim went with Betty and her husband to the game. Just before the quarterback threw the game-winning touchdown in the last minute, Tina stood up and yelled, "Go, Richie!" Chris, Willy, and Jill were sure that they heard her on TV.

THE END

18

Chris knew it was hopeless. He would never catch the kid. He looked at the old woman—and wondered. What was her story? Why was she here begging for quarters?

Suddenly Chris remembered a story from the Bible that Miss Whitehead once told—the one about getting to heaven and meeting Jesus. In the story, Jesus welcomed a group of people by saying, "Thank you. When I was hungry, you fed me. When I was thirsty, you gave me a drink." And the people were surprised because they never remembered meeting Jesus or caring for his needs. And Jesus pointed to the poor people of the world and said, "Whatever you have done for these people, my brothers and sisters, you've done for me."

Chris looked at the old woman again and felt something funny tugging at his insides. She could use a lot of things, but all she asked him for was a quarter. *"When I was hungry, you fed me. . . . "*

Chris nodded to himself and shoved his hand into his pocket. He pulled out two quarters and pressed them into the woman's well-worn hand. "Here," he said. "Here's fifty cents. Betty can give you a Coke for that. She's pretty nice. Maybe she'll even give you some ice cream."

The woman's eyes showed no emotion as she clutched the two quarters in her fist.

"Do you want to come into the Freeze with me?" Chris

offered. He shuddered to think of how his friends might tease him, but he knew this was right.

"No," she said. "Gotta go. Get a burger."

"All right," Chris answered. "That's fine. Get a burger. The Maple Diner has good ones, but that'll cost you more. That's just down this road."

The woman was poking around in her big handbag. "You help me, I help you," she muttered. "You help me, I help you. You help me, I help you." It was like a song.

Chris was getting nervous. The woman was acting strange. He backed away, toward the Freeze.

Just then, she pulled a small piece of cardboard out of her bag and held it toward him. "I help you," she said proudly. Cautiously, Chris took it from her. It was the missing ticket.

"How did you . . . ?"

The woman kept muttering as she walked away, "Heh, heh, heh. That Sonny. You'll never catch him. Lots of loot, that boy. Never catch him."

"I don't know!" Chris said for the millionth time as he and the other boys sat in the stands at Robert F. Kennedy Memorial Stadium. "I think she knew the kid! He must have given her the ticket to hold on to. That way, if I caught him, I wouldn't have any proof that he stole it."

"Sounds good," said Pete. "But where did the kid go?"

"I'm telling you—he vanished into thin air!"

"You know what I think?" said Sam, pausing to sip his drink. "I think they were angels."

"Go 'Skins!" yelled Willy as the team came out on the

20

field. The whole stadium went bonkers as each player was introduced.

THE END

Chris and Willy stood their ground. The two men came toward them.

"You may wonder what we're doing here," Chris began. Before he could say another word, the men nabbed them by their collars and hauled them into the coach's office.

The coach called security while the other man grilled the boys. "We'll get your little friend later," he said.

"He's not our friend," Chris began to explain.

"I don't care how your little thievery ring operates," the man snapped. "I just want you to return what you stole."

"But we didn't steal anything!" Willy protested.

"Do you know these kids?" the man asked the coach.

Coach Winston looked them over. "Not the white one, but the black boy looks familiar. How did you boys get in here? We're all locked up."

"We crawled under the fence," Chris said.

"Very clever," the other man said. "Now where are the tickets?"

The two boys looked at each other. Then Chris spoke. "We didn't have tickets, sir. That's why we had to crawl under the fence."

The security men showed up at the door. Immediately, one was ordered to hunt down the other little kid. The other guard recognized Chris and Willy and broke into a sharp, sadistic smile. "I'm glad you caught these two," he said. "They're troublemakers."

"You've dealt with them before?" the coach asked.

"Chased them halfway around the stadium this morning," the guard said. "I'm still catching my breath."

"But you lost them," the other man snapped.

The guard glared at the two boys. "The little rascals ran off into the woods."

"We did not," Chris shouted. "There was a hole under the fence. We crawled through."

Willy kicked Chris. "Don't tell them," he whispered. "They'll find the hole."

Then everyone started talking at once. The man was saying how incompetent the guards were. The guard was saying how bad the boys were. The boys were arguing about whether they should tell how they got in. Finally, the coach blew his whistle, and everyone stopped.

"Now let's sort this out," Coach Winston commanded. "Officer, about what time did you chase the suspects?"

"It was oh-nine-forty, sir."

"Sounds like a tennis score. Can you speak English?"

"Twenty to ten, sir."

"All right. And, Mr. Myers," he said to the other man, "when did we discover the tickets were missing?"

"It was nine o'clock, Jack."

The coach went on to figure out that the tickets were stolen before the boys even got there. "All right, boys, you're free to go—home. Officer, take them outside the stadium."

But before he went anywhere, the other guard was carrying in the nine-year-old. "I found him trying to watch the practice from under the stands."

"Does he have any tickets on him?" the coach asked.

"No," said the guard. "I searched him, and all I found was a pad and pencil and this." He handed the coach a white card.

"It's a press pass. For Daniel Wright."

The other man's eyes widened. "A sportswriter for the *Post*. Where did you get that?"

"That's my dad," the boy said, almost in tears. "He gave it to me. He wanted me to sneak in and get a story."

The coach was shaking his head. "Imagine that."

The other man smiled for the first time. "That's why he's the best sportswriter in D.C."

The coach ordered the guard to usher the boy out as well. "Well, I guess the only story you're going to get, my boy, is on how good the security is around here."

As the guards left, the other man pounded the desk, crying, "And I'm still left with five thousand missing tickets!"

Five steps down the hall, Willy stopped in his tracks. "Did he say five thousand missing tickets? Come on, Chris. We may be able to help after all."

Chris and Willy went back into the office and reported the conversation they overheard between the candy manager and his girlfriend.

"Of course!" the coach said. "Greg used to be our team manager. He would have had keys to all these offices. I bet he's the thief."

The story appeared in the paper the next day, written

24

by "Dan Wright." Chris and Willy knew it was his son, Joey, who *really* got the story.

The other man in the office apologized to Chris and Willy for being so nasty. His name was Steve Myers, and he worked for the Redskins' public relations office. He gave each of the boys a Redskins jersey and even introduced them to some of the players—including Reggie Sanders and Deacon Joe Johnson. By the time the boys left, they felt like they were members of the team.

The boys thanked Mr. Myers and said good-bye. That was when Mr. Myers handed them free tickets to the season opener. "Now make sure no one steals them," he said with a grin. They laughed.

THE END

Stolen tickets. Underground tickets. Extra tickets. Missing tickets. Have you gotten them all? If not, turn to page 34 and make different choices along the way.

Jill was face-to-face with the ugliest face she had ever seen. The eyes were bloodshot, the forehead badly wrinkled, the nose was long and crooked, the cheeks and chin had pimples and scars. Gray and black hair stuck out from the head, looking like it hadn't been combed for days. The mouth was open, revealing teeth that were yellow and decaying. The creature was letting out an eerie high-pitched wail.

It was a woman, dressed in a ratty housedress. A moment earlier, she had been poking through a trash can that was chained to the tree. But then Jill came flying toward her, scaring her as much as Jill herself was scared. Both let out a surprised scream. As they caught their breath, Tina came rushing to help Jill. When she saw the creature, she too let out a scream, which set the strange woman screaming more.

Jill grabbed her friend's hand. "Let's get out of here—quick!" They rushed out of the Common and dashed across the street to the Freeze, quickly claiming the two counter stools farthest from the door.

Betty Metz turned from the shelves she was stocking. "Hello, girls!" was her cheery welcome. But then she noticed their wide eyes and rapid breathing. "What happened to you two? You look like you've seen a ghost."

"You might say that," said Jill. "Who *was* that woman?"

"What woman?" Betty asked. Jill described her frightening experience, but Betty couldn't explain it. Jill even led Betty to the front window, but the strange woman had vanished. "I don't know, girls," Betty laughed. "Maybe it's the Ghost of Millersburg Common."

"You really think so?" asked Jill.

Tina shook her head. "My dad says there's no such thing as ghosts."

"Well, then," said Betty, walking over to the cash register to ring up a customer, "listen to your dad, 'cause he's a lot smarter than I'll ever be."

"Wait a second," Jill argued. "What about the Holy Ghost? Your dad should certainly know about that 'cause he's a missionary."

With a *r-r-ring* of the register, Betty opened the cash drawer and handed out some change. Tina thought a moment and argued back. "But he's not really a ghost, he's a spir—"

"Jill, my girl," Betty interrupted, suddenly taking on a motherly tone. "Never start a theology argument with a missionary kid. You can't win."

They all smiled. Betty turned to call out a good-bye to the customers who were leaving. Just then, she noticed a little boy slipping in the door. He was shabbily dressed and had a serious look on his face. The boy scampered over to the table the customers had just left. As Betty walked back to the girls, she saw him sip from one of the water glasses they had left on the table. She frowned but didn't say anything.

"Girls, I have just the thing to get your minds off your

harrowing experience," Betty said. She waved an envelope in front of them. "How do you feel about football?"

"Not football again!" Tina moaned. Jill moaned with her.

Betty explained that a salesman had come through that morning, leaving her with six tickets to the Redskins' first preseason game the next weekend. She and her husband could use two of them, but she had four extras for any of the Ringers who were interested.

"So I thought that maybe you, Tina, could bring your brother; and you, Jill, could bring Chris."

"Chris—ugh," Jill groaned.

Betty looked surprised. "Did I say something wrong?"

"*Chris* said something wrong," Jill explained. "He's just so . . . so . . . so *male,*" she said with a scowl.

"Yes." Betty smiled. "I've noticed that's a problem."

"He wouldn't let us play football with the boys this morning," Tina added.

"I see. Well, what about your brother, Tina?"

"He's away at a church camp this week and next, having fun."

Now Betty was nodding. "And you're left back here being bored, right? Well, it seems like you both have a chance to turn the tables. Tina can have some fun while her brother's at camp, and you both can choose anyone you want to go with you to the game." Betty counted out the four tickets and placed them on the counter. "There are only four tickets. You decide who's going, and I'll call your folks to make the arrangements."

28

A while later, the front door clanged open and four tired-looking boys walked in.

"It's hot," Pete mumbled.

"You bet," Willy agreed.

"Too hot for football, that's for sure," Sam added.

"Yeah," said Chris. "Whose idea was it to play football anyway?"

"Yours!" said all the others, as they piled into a corner booth.

"Who won?" asked Betty, putting four glasses of water on the counter.

"It was a tie," said Sam, getting up for the water.

"Nothing to nothing," added Pete.

"We got to Willy's and just didn't want to play," Chris explained.

"It was too hot," said Willy with a nod.

"The girls have a surprise for you," Betty teased.

"Shhhhhh, Betty!" said Jill. "Maybe we shouldn't tell them."

"Tell us what?" the boys were asking.

Jill was still unsure. "What do you think?" she whispered to Tina. "Should we tell them about the tickets?"

"I don't know," Tina said quietly.

CHOICE ⇒

If the girls tell the boys about the tickets, turn to page 77.

If the girls keep quiet about it, turn to page 93.

Chris thought about the surprise that Betty had promised. And he thought about Willy, who had been his friend for a long time. He felt that he probably should stay with Willy, but there wasn't much he could do for him, was there? Willy would be fine. Besides, his mom and dad would be home soon.

"I guess I'll go with the others," Chris finally said. They said their good-byes to Willy and trooped over to the Freeze, their favorite ice-cream hangout. The manager, Betty Metz, enjoyed having the Ringers around. She said they made her feel young again.

"Hi, kids!" she called as they walked into the place and claimed a row of counter stools. Looking at Pete, she said, "I thought you forgot all about my surprise today."

"I almost did," he said sheepishly.

"So what's the surprise, Betty?" the others were asking. "Free ice cream?"

"Don't you wish!" she laughed. "Actually, it's something even better."

"Better than ice cream?" Sam said in mock disbelief.

"Early this morning," Betty explained, "just before you came in, Pete, a man came by offering free tickets to the Redskins game next Saturday. It's the preseason opener. He gave me six—two for me and my husband, and I took four for you guys."

30

The kids were very excited, all except Tina. She knew how to count.

"But there are five of us here, and we can't forget Willy."

"I was afraid of that," said Betty. "I should have asked for more."

"No that's fine," Pete assured her. "We'll figure this out. We're just glad that some of us can go."

Meanwhile, Willy sat in the easy chair in his living room, his feet on a footstool, spaced out. The injury had taken a lot out of him.

Then the phone rang. *Why isn't Chris getting that for me?* he thought, then realized Chris wasn't there. The phone rang again, jarring Willy back into the real world. The phone was on a table just a few steps away from the chair. Slowly, Willy put his feet on the floor and stood. His ankle had stiffened up. It felt weird, even though he wasn't putting his full weight on it. He hopped over to the phone and answered it. It was his mom.

"Oh, I'm fine," Willy said without thinking. "What's up?"

His mom needed a phone number from a paper that was hanging on the refrigerator door. Without thinking, Willy stepped toward the kitchen—on the bad ankle. It couldn't support him. He twisted it again and fell down.

Fortunately, he still had the phone in his hand. "Uh, Mom," he said from the floor, "remember when I said I was fine? I lied."

Mrs. Washington hurried home and took Willy to the doctor. They learned that Willy had seriously sprained his ankle. It was probably just a minor twist at first, the doctor said, but he should have stopped playing immediately. Now he would have to be off his feet for two weeks.

When Chris found out about this, he felt awful. Since Willy wouldn't be able to go to the game, and Chris felt partly to blame, Chris gave up his chance for a ticket. That left four tickets for four Ringers.

The night of the game, Chris and Willy watched the action on TV, looking for their friends in the stands. It was a thrilling victory by the Redskins. The quarterback threw a touchdown pass in the last minute to win it. At that moment, Chris and Willy threw popcorn in the air (which Chris had to pick up). After the game, Betty and her husband drove over to Willy's apartment, bringing the other four Ringers—and several pints of ice cream. They had a splendid victory party, one they wouldn't soon forget.

CHOICE ➤

If you haven't found out who the Worths are, turn to page 34 and make different choices along the way. Or turn to page 124.

It's up to me to start the niceness. That phrase turned around a few times in Jill's mind. With these tickets, she had a great chance to teach these boys a lesson. But, in a way, it would just be a way to get even, to make them squirm for the grief they had caused the girls.

Suddenly she thought of her Social Studies class. She had learned about the wars in Ireland and Lebanon and South Africa and Iraq. It seemed as if there were fighting all over the world. *And why?* It seemed so pointless. *I shoot you because you shot my brother, who shot your brother, who shot . . .* Jill shook her head sadly. Countries acted just like little kids.

"It's up to *you* to start the niceness." What if everyone said that? No one would *ever* stop fighting!

Jill made a decision. "Tina," she finally whispered, "do you really want to go to this game?"

Tina shrugged. "Not really."

Jill grinned. She knew the boys were going to freak when she told them what she'd decided. And she knew it was the right decision to make. "OK," she said, nudging Tina in the arm. "Let's go start the niceness."

They strolled back to the booth where the boys were waiting. "We have made our decision concerning the tickets," she announced. She reached into her right pocket, but the ticket envelope wasn't there. "Uh . . . ," she repeated, going to her left hip pocket, "concerning the *tickets* . . . " They weren't there, either. "Tina!" she whispered. "Where are the tickets?"

Tina went back to the counter. There was the small white envelope, with tickets partly showing. She brought it back to Jill.

"It's like this," Jill went on, sighing with relief. "We got to thinking, *Who would enjoy this football game the most?*"

"I would!" said Chris, reaching for a ticket.

"No, I would!" shouted Willy, reaching past Chris (Willy's arms were longer).

Jill held the tickets away from them. "Tina and I enjoy the finer things in life," she said. "We'll let you boys watch grown men in pads run into each other." Then she began to lay the tickets neatly on the table. "One. Two. Three. Where's four?"

She frantically turned the envelope inside out. "Betty," she called. "I thought you said there were four tickets here!"

"There were when I gave them to you," Betty answered.

Tina was near tears. "I guess somebody stole it."

They looked around the Freeze for a moment. Suddenly, the door jangled open and a little boy darted out.

"I bet he took it!" Chris shouted.

CHOICE ➡

If Chris runs after the boy, turn to page 86.

If they decide to call the police, turn to page 67.

"**W**ait!" he said, putting his index fingers to his forehead, as if he were some kind of mind reader. "I know where they are."

"Where? Where?" the others were asking.

Sam sheepishly reached into his back pocket. "Right here, guys," he said, producing the stack of cards. "Sorry. I forgot."

"Sometimes I think you put your brain back there," Chris laughed. Soon they were all laughing as they walked away.

"What do you wanna do?"

"I don't know. What do you wanna do?"

Sam was unusually quiet. Suddenly he said, "What if they put out 'people cards'?"

"What?" the other three said, all at the same time.

"The heat is finally getting to Sam's mind," said Willy.

"People cards," he explained, ignoring Willy. "Just like baseball or football cards, except they'd have people like you and me. What kind of stuff would they put on the back?"

"Maybe like how you're doing in school," Pete suggested.

"Yuk!" said Willy.

"Or maybe how good a person you are," Chris added. "Good deeds you do, stuff like that."

"Yeah," Willy thought out loud. "Just think of what Miss Whitehead's 'people card' would say."

They all paused for a moment, remembering their old Sunday school teacher. She had died about a year earlier, but she had made a lasting impression on the boys. With her love and attention and simple wisdom, she had made each of them feel very special.

"Hi, guys!"

"How ya doing?"

Those voices could only come from the two female members of the "Ringers"—Tina and Jill. It was kind of funny that they showed up at that moment because Tina was Miss Whitehead's grandniece. Tina's parents were missionaries in Brazil, and she had recently moved back to Virginia with her grandparents. Her grandfather, Miss Whitehead's twin brother, was trying to reopen the old Capitol Community Church.

Jill was Chris's cousin. She was staying with Chris's family for the summer. Both girls were just thirteen, a year younger than the guys. They often joined the boys on their adventures, but sometimes they just went off and did their own things. Chris was glad that Tina was around for Jill to be friends with. At first, he was afraid that Jill would be pestering him all summer. Who wants a girl cousin tagging along? But she hit it off right away with Tina, and the boys seemed to like her, too. Chris had to admit, Jill was sometimes pretty cool. But other times, she was . . . she was . . . well, she was a *girl*.

"What's up?" Jill was asking.

"Sky," said Chris.

"Clouds," said Willy.

"Temperature," said Sam, mopping sweat off of his forehead.

"Ha, ha. You guys are hysterical," Tina piped up. "Really, what are you doing?"

Chris looked down at the card in his hand and got an idea. "We were just heading over to Willy's apartment to play some football. Right, Will?"

"We were?" Willy asked. Chris shoved an elbow into his side. "Oh, yeah, we were! I could get my football out of the garage, and we could play in the field behind the apartment."

"Tackle or touch?" asked Pete. He was the tallest of the group, but the least athletic. His body always seemed to get a little bigger than he was used to as he grew, and that made him kind of clumsy. He would reach for a pass, and the ball would usually hit him in the wrists.

"We'd better play touch," said Sam.

Willy moaned. "Awww! Touch is for sissies. Let's play tackle!"

"Yeah," Sam answered, "but if the girls are playing—"

"We can play tackle," said Jill. "Right, Tina? We're tough enough."

Tina wasn't sure at all. But she figured the girls had better stick together, so she nodded. "Right. We're tough."

"No," Chris said firmly. "Girls can't play. Whoever heard of girls playing football?"

"Let's play touch anyway," said Pete. I don't want to get hurt."

"Me, neither," Sam added.

"Well," Tina chirped, "if you insist—"

"No!" Chris repeated. "The girls aren't playing. Touch *or* tackle—I don't want to play football with girls. Come on, guys, aren't you with me on this?"

Willy and Sam and Pete thought about it. They all knew that Chris got weird about the girls sometimes. After all, Jill was his cousin, and Chris had told them how, when they were little, she used to mess up kickball games. But that was then and this was now. The girls weren't messing up the games anymore. They added to the fun—usually. As Willy and Sam and Pete thought about it, they realized that they really liked these girls—not *liked,* you understand—but they were kind of fun to be with.

Still, Chris felt strongly about this. And the football game was his idea. And without him, there wouldn't be much of a game (since Chris and Willy were the best players). And shouldn't the boys stick together on important things?

All of these thoughts went through their mind in a few seconds. Soon each of the boys had made up his mind.

CHOICE ⟾

If they let the girls play, turn to page 73.

If they *don't* let the girls play, turn to page 60.

If they can't decide, turn to page 50.

38

"This leads to the coaches' offices," Willy said, as they ventured through another hallway.

"What was that guy up to?" asked Chris.

"I don't know," Willy replied. "But it didn't sound good."

"He was selling five thousand of something. Something pretty expensive. I wonder what it was."

Suddenly, as they walked along, they heard more voices. "Hit the dirt!" Willy said.

"I don't see how you can be so irresponsible," said one voice. "That will cost us a bundle—at least in community goodwill."

"I know," said another. It was an older, tired voice. "We'll do all we can to locate—"

"You'd better! We have a contract with this school, and that's based on trust. No trust, no contract."

"I understand. I'm sorry. We'll take care of it."

Chris was pulling on Willy's sleeve. "Who's that?"

"The one getting yelled at sounds like Coach Winston. He's the athletic director here. I don't know the other guy."

The "other guy" was ranting on. "I'd hate to get the police involved in this. Or the press. Imagine what they'd do with this story! But we are talking grand larceny, not petty theft."

Just then, the ceiling caved in—well, it seemed like it.

An air vent in the hallway ceiling suddenly lost its grating, and a little boy, about nine or ten years old, fell out. He landed on his feet and ran down the hall.

The men in the office were surprised. "What in—!" Coach Winston began.

"I bet that's our thief," said the other man, as they hurried out to the hall.

The boy rushed past Chris and Willy. They were frozen. Should they run after him, or stay and state their case?

CHOICE

If they run after the boy, turn to page 56.

If they stay and try to reason with the men, turn to page 21.

Sam grabbed the candle and turned toward the other tunnel. At the last second, he snatched up the tickets that were lying on the old suitcase. He figured Jill might like to have those back.

A high-pitched wail from the other tunnel made him move faster—away from the hole in the ground, on to who-knew-where. Stuffing the tickets in his pocket, he held a hand in front of the candle to keep it from blowing out. He had to hunch over a little, but he didn't have to crawl.

Soon, in the candle's light he saw that the tunnel came to a dead end. A large piece of plywood blocked the way.

"Beautiful!" Sam mumbled. "Not only do I walk out on my friends and run into a tree and fall into a hole, but I'm going to rot here in a dead-end tunnel—unless of course I'm eaten by this creature from the black lagoon." He tried to make a joke of it, as always. But he was really worried.

He began to pray for rescue. He knew what Chris would say: "You just have to trust God. God will help you out."

Oh, how Sam wished he could be tossing a football with Chris right then, and with Willy and Pete, and even the girls! He was with them all just an hour ago, but then one thing after another, and here he was with his life passing before his eyes. "I'm so young," he said out loud, in kind of a choked-up voice, "I'll have to call for a rerun."

But there was no one to hear his joke, no one to laugh. He felt very much alone. "OK, God," Sam prayed, "you gotta help me. There's nothing more I can do."

Dejected, he sat down at the end of the tunnel, leaning back against the plywood.

It moved.

Turn to page 47.

The next morning, Willy tested out his ankle. It felt a bit stiff, but it was stronger than before. He wrapped it in the Ace bandage and took a few more steps. It felt good. He put on his socks and shoes. He paced across his room. He was going to be fine. "All right!" he cheered to himself.

Chris showed up at nine. "Ready for the Redskins?" he asked.

"You bet!" said Willy with a huge grin. He limped a few steps in place to show Chris how healthy his ankle was.

"Well, it's you and me, buddy."

Willy looked upset. "Sam and Pete aren't coming?"

"No. Sam had some chores to do, and Pete chickened out."

"What about the girls?"

"They say they don't like football that much."

"*Now* they tell us!"

Chris and Willy laughed together. "It's probably just as well," Chris said. "It's easier for two to sneak around than six. How are we getting there?"

"Zeke. He's headed for the college library anyway."

Zeke dropped the boys off near the gate to the college stadium. Two security guards stood there in their crisp blue uniforms. The gate was padlocked, and a chain-link fence surrounded the stadium area. In the distance the boys heard a sound of grunting, in a steady

beat. *UH—uh—uh—uh—UH—uh—uh—uh* . . .
Something was going on inside, but they couldn't see the
field because the stands were in the way. And those guards
weren't letting anyone in.

"Let's try the end zone," Willy whispered. They tried
to move as innocently as possible around the stadium.

One of the guards saw them. "Hey you! Come here!"

"What should we do?" Willy whispered.

"Run!" Chris whispered back.

"On this ankle? They'd catch me for sure! Maybe
they'll leave us alone if we talk to them."

"I don't think so," Chris said doubtfully.

CHOICE

If the boys run, turn to page 96.

If the boys stay and play innocent, turn to page 44.

Though Chris objected, Willy went limping toward the guards. Chris had to follow. "Good morning, officers! Is there any problem?"

The gruff guards seemed a bit surprised by Willy's politeness. "You're not supposed to be around here."

"Oh, I'm sorry," Chris said, coming up behind Willy. "I guess we're in the wrong place, Matt. Didn't your dad say to come to the front gate?"

Willy was picking up on Chris's game now. "Uh, yes, Harry. That's what I thought my father said. He was going to clear it with the guards."

The guards seemed unmoved.

Chris turned back to the security officers. "You're sure that Deacon Joe didn't say anything about his son coming today?"

"Nope," barked the guard.

"It's a shame," Chris went on, turning back to Willy, "because he really wanted you to see him play—even in practice. And with you going to the boarding school next week, you may not be able to."

"Yeah," Willy agreed. "And this being his last season and all. That's really sad. I thought for sure he said to come to the stadium gate."

"Maybe we can wait. Maybe Deacon Joe hasn't had a chance to talk to these guards yet."

"Of course he won't be very happy that they made us wait."

Chris tried to "calm down" his friend. "Now, Matt, they're just doing their job."

"Yeah, but I hate to see my dad get mad. He can get really mean."

"And he's three-hundred pounds."

"Three-fifty."

The guards were beginning to fidget. "Uh, how do we know you're Deacon Joe's son?"

Willy was stumped, but Chris saved the day. He pulled a football card from his back pocket. "Who else would carry a football card of Deacon Joe everywhere he goes?" Chris said, handing the card to Willy. "Thanks for letting me see it, Matt."

One guard took the card and examined it.

"And you see," Chris added, "where it says, 'Children: Matt, 14; Darlene, 12'? You know, Matt, it's a shame Dar couldn't come with us today."

The guard growled at Chris, "Who are you?"

"I'm Matt's best friend, Henry."

"Harry," Willy corrected him quickly.

Chris didn't miss a beat. "Harry! That's what everyone calls me. We grew up together."

"In Minnesota?" asked the second guard, who was now reading the card. "Says here the Deacon used to play for the Vikings."

"Yes." Chris nodded. "It sure was cold there. *Brrr!*"

The two boys shivered. They were beginning to realize this story of theirs was heading toward a dead end.

46

"What's your last name?" the first guard asked.

"Uh, Tarkenton. Harry Tarkenton. Pleased to meet you." He put out his hand for a shake but got a cold stare.

"And you both moved here to Washington?" asked the second guard.

"We're very close," said Willy, putting his arm around Chris's shoulders.

The guards put their heads together briefly, as the boys sweated it out.

"Nice try, kids," said the second guard. "But I happen to know Deacon Joe. He's not mean at all. His family still lives in Minnesota, and his son isn't going to any boarding school."

"So whoever you are," the first guard added, "get lost."

Chris and Willy skulked away, dejected. They found their way to the library and got Zeke to drive them home. Their sneaky adventure was not to be.

THE END

If you think a sneaky adventure is a bad idea anyway, turn to page 34 and try other choices.

Sam inspected the plywood. By leaning against it, he had pushed it off of a supporting bar. In a moment he was up and prying at the wood. He quickly saw that there were two pieces of wood. The smaller one was pretty easy to move, opening a hole big enough for Sam to step through.

On the other side of the plywood was a room with paneled walls and a firm floor, not just another dirt tunnel (which Sam was getting sick of). There was something familiar about the room. Sam walked slowly—ten, eleven, twelve paces to the other wall. There was something hanging there: a plaque. Holding the candle up to it, Sam read, "Thank you, Lord, for saving me."

Sam smiled—his first smile in almost an hour. "I couldn't have said it better myself." Looking up, he said, "Thanks." And suddenly he knew where he was—in the church. He'd been in another one of those crazy tunnels under the church that the Ringers had discovered before. They never realized that there was another tunnel, this one leading out to the Common.

Quickly, Sam traced the familiar path up to the main floor of the church. He raced into Mr. Whitehead's office, where he found him with a man he didn't know and five kids he knew all too well—the Ringers. They all looked up with surprise.

"Where have you been? How did you get here? What happened to you? Are you all right?"

Sam had to field a million questions. He tried to explain about the tunnels and the hole in the Common.

"We'll have to get that patched up," said Mr. Whitehead, with a nod to the strange man. "That could be dangerous."

"I'll say!" murmured Sam.

Mr. Whitehead continued. "You know, I bet that's another holdover from the Underground Railroad. They probably hid slaves in the basement, then sneaked them out of town even when the church was being watched. I bet they had it patched up, but the patching just gave way."

"Oh," said Sam, "I almost forgot." He fished the tickets out of his pocket and offered them to Jill with a flourish. "You might be missing these. Or maybe I shouldn't give them to you unless you're very nice to me."

Jill looked puzzled. "That's very nice, Sam, but—" She pulled four tickets from her own pocket. "I still have my tickets."

Sam looked at her, shocked, his eyes bugging out. "Then whose are these?"

The strange man was now looking over Sam's shoulder at the tickets. "They look like mine," he said. "You seen my boy?"

"Your boy?"

Mr. Whitehead explained. "This is Mr. Worth. He's from the city, and he's going to be doing some work for us around the church. He's here with his son and with his elderly mother. You may have seen them today in the church or on the Common."

Jill and Tina looked at each other. "You mean *that's* the woman we saw in the Common?"

"And this morning a man from the Washington Redskins came by, handing out free tickets to next week's game. He gave us four, which we let Sonny hold for us."

Just then, a small boy of seven or eight darted into the room and between the others. Deftly, he grabbed the tickets from Sam's hand. In a high-pitched whine, he said, "Those are *mine.*"

Suddenly Sam realized this was the "creature" from the tunnel. "I–I'm sorry," he stuttered. "I didn't know. I was afraid."

The boy took a position partially behind his father. "*You* were afraid?" he said softly.

Mr. Worth cleared his throat and announced, "Look, I've got an idea. I'm not one for football, and my mother isn't either. Why don't we give two of those tickets to you young folks, and you can all go with the Reverend and my boy?"

The gang could hardly believe it. What a way to wrap up an already adventurous summer!

THE END

It was Pete who broke the silence. "Well, I think the girls ought to play if they want. I mean, they've been on a lot of adventures with us this summer and all."

"Yeah," Sam agreed. "Let 'em play."

Chris wasn't buying it. "But this is football, man! It's a man's sport. You don't see girls out there playing with the Redskins. Right, Willy?"

At that moment Willy wasn't sure of anything. He hated disagreements, especially among friends. He had heard his parents arguing sometimes, late at night, and it bothered him a lot. But Chris was his best buddy, and he was counting on him. He had to stand with his friend, didn't he?

"I'm with Chris," Willy said softly.

"There you have it," Chris announced. "Two to two. We're tied."

"Wait!" snapped Jill. "What are we? Chopped liver?"

Sam held back a laugh. "Wellll . . ." he started to say. The girls were not amused.

"It looks like four to two, the way I count it," Jill continued.

"But you're girls," Chris protested.

"So we don't count! Is that what you're trying to say?"

Tina was tugging at Jill's sleeve, but Jill went on, ranting about women earning the right to vote. She had

done a report on that in her social studies class the
previous year. It had been a great speech, about the value
of each individual person. Tina kept tugging at her sleeve,
and Jill kept talking. Chris looked down at the ground and
nodded. Willy was thinking about the Redskins and about
how much he hated arguments.

When Jill stopped to breathe, Sam burst into
applause. She just gave him a hurt look.

"Uh, Jill?" It was Tina, tapping Jill on the shoulder.

"What is it, Tina?" asked Jill, looking rather annoyed.

"I really don't feel like playing football after all."

So it was still tied, three to three.

Finally, "What do you want to do?" one of them asked.

"I don't know. What do you want to do?"

"Nothin'."

And that was just the kind of day it was!

CHOICE ⇛

What a drag of a day! Turn to page 34, and try a
different option.

Jill looked around, expecting all the others to leave, too. *This is like a bad TV show,* she couldn't help thinking. But no one else left. Finally, she spoke. "OK, so maybe that wasn't such a great idea."

Tina giggled nervously.

Meanwhile, Sam was striding across the Common. He wasn't sure where he was going. He just needed to get out of there. Sometimes he got sick of all this you're-not-nice-enough garbage. Why couldn't friends just be friends and quit playing games?

He watched his feet pound the green grass. *This day has not been a good one,* he thought. Spilled soda pop, a football game that didn't happen, a fight at the Freeze. What else could go wrong?

He walked into a tree.

Not head-on or anything, but it caught his shoulder, giving him a nasty bruise. He had been staring down, not watching where he was going, and suddenly a burly oak tree was standing there in front of him. He winced from the pain and looked around to see if anyone had noticed. No one.

Great, he thought. *Spilled soda, "Only Two Kids Permitted," no football, heat so bad you can cut it with a knife, a dumb disagreement at the Freeze—and now I'm attacked by an oak tree. I might as well go to bed right now, before anything worse happens.*

Just then, the church bell began to ring. Sam looked at it curiously. It was three in the afternoon. The church bell *never* rang at three in the afternoon. The rich sound bounced against the buildings and echoed through the Common. Suddenly, Sam thought he heard his name. As the echo surrounded him, he heard, "Sam! Sam!" He looked up at the old Capitol Community Church. The doors were open.

He felt better already. He remembered how the church had been closed up for years, but now Mr. Whitehead—Tina and Jim's grandfather—was there to reopen it. Already the Ringers had helped get that bell working again.

That's what I'll do, he thought. *I'll go to the church. That will make me feel better.*

Once again he was marching across the grassy common, but he wasn't angry anymore. He kept his eye on the church every step of the way, daydreaming about the underground passages they had found there.

Suddenly he was falling. He had daydreamed his way right into a hole in the middle of the Common.

The ten-foot-deep hole was new. He had no idea why it was there in the middle of the Common. It had not been roped off or marked at all, and Sam had never seen it. One moment there was grass beneath his feet, then there was nothing. He found himself looking up at a small patch of blue sky. Around him there was only dirt. The fall—and the surprise—had knocked the wind out of him. He struggled to breathe.

Wonderful! he thought. *Spilled soda, the dumb store, forgetting the football cards, no football game, terrible heat, the stupid stuff at the Freeze, running into a tree—and now being buried alive. This is not my day.* He rubbed his shoulder stiffly. *There must be a lesson in all this.* But he couldn't figure out what it was.

He heard the voice again. "Sam! Sam!" Then a face blocked out the blue sky above him. It was Pete.

"Sam! What are you doing down there?"

"Oh, I don't know. I'm beating the heat. It's cooler down here. You ought to try it."

"But didn't you hear me calling you? Why didn't you stop?"

"Oh, that was you?"

"Of course! Who did you think it was?"

"Never mind. Do you think you can get me up out of this hole?"

Pete reached his long arms down to Sam, but they couldn't quite make the connection.

"Maybe you ought to go get some help," Sam finally suggested.

"You think I should?"

"Well, *I'd* do it," Sam responded, "but I'm kind of busy right now."

"I mean, I wouldn't want to embarrass you or anything. Maybe if I lean forward a little more . . ."

CHOICE ⟹

If Pete goes to get help, turn to page 110.

If Pete stays and tries harder, turn to page 114.

They ran. Ahead of them there was a door swinging. The boy must have passed through there. They went through it—into another hallway. Glancing to their left, they noticed a flash of movement at the end of the hall. The boy! They followed.

"Uh, Willy," said Chris, gasping for air as they ran. "Why are we chasing this kid?"

"I don't know. It's fun."

"But if he's in trouble, then we'll be in trouble, too."

"You've got a point there. But who is he?"

CHOICE ⇒

If Chris and Willy keep chasing the boy, turn to page 90.

If Chris and Willy stop chasing, turn to page 106.

"**C**ome on, Tina," said Chris. "What's that secret all about?"

Tina was embarrassed by the sudden attention. "I . . . uh . . . I don't think I should tell." At her side, Jill smiled proudly.

"Tell you what. We'll all chip in and buy you some ice cream. How would you like that?"

"We will?" Willy asked. Chris jabbed him in the ribs. "Oh yeah," Willy said, recovering. "We'll all chip in." Then he whispered to Chris, "But I don't have any money. I spent my last change on that soda."

"Uh . . . I don't know," said Tina, with a quick glance in Jill's direction.

"Just think about it, Tina," Chris continued. "A big, heaping dish of mint chocolate chip ice cream—"

Tina made a face.

"I mean *chocolate* ice cream."

"*Double* chocolate," Sam volunteered.

"Yeah, double chocolate," Chris added. "Forget that mint stuff. A cool, refreshing bowl of frozen delight on this very hot day. And it's all yours if you just tell us the secret."

"That's bribery!" Jill protested. "Hang in there, Tina. Hold out long enough and they'll buy you a new bike."

"Come on, Tina," begged Willy. "After Jill told you that crazy story about the grass, I don't know why you're on her side about this. I mean, you wanted to tell us earlier, right?"

"Well, I wanted to tell because I thought we'd have to give the tickets out right away, but—" Suddenly she realized she had said too much.

"Tickets?" Chris asked. "Did I hear something about tickets?"

Jill frowned, then sighed. "You might as well tell them now," she told Tina.

Tina explained how Betty had given them some tickets to a Redskins game. The boys listened with interest, then looked at each other.

"Come on," said Sam. "What's the *real* secret?"

"That's it," said Jill. "Honest."

"Look who's saying, 'Honest'," Chris crowed. "After that grass story, do you really expect us to fall for this ticket thing? *Nobody* gets tickets to Redskins games. Nice try."

"But it's true!" Jill cried. "Look, I have the tickets right here." She reached into her right pocket, then her left pocket, then her back pockets. "Oh, I must have left them back at the counter."

The small white envelope was there, but no tickets. "Somebody took them!" she said. "Somebody stole our tickets!"

The boys were laughing as they got up and prepared to leave. "That's good, Jill. We almost believed you. What an actress! Ha! Tickets to a Redskins game! And I'm Julius Caesar!"

"Betty can tell you it's true! Betty! Tell them what happened!"

But Betty was waiting on a customer. "Not now, dear," she answered.

The boys filed out the door, still chuckling over Jill's story. "See you later," they said. "We're going to hang out at Sam's house for a while."

Halfway across the Common, Sam pulled four tickets out of his pocket. "How long before I tell her I took them?"

"Give her about five more minutes," Chris suggested. "Then we'll go back."

"You know," Pete said, "this is really cruel."

"Well, they were sitting right there on the counter when I got my water," Sam answered. "I couldn't resist."

"Uh-oh," said Willy.

"What's wrong?" the others responded.

"We've been walking on the African grass with . . . *with our shoes on!*"

"Oh no!" Chris yelled. "The Gas Grass! We're doomed!"

All four began to stagger around as if they were fainting. They collapsed on the ground in laughter.

CHOICE ⇒

Is this the end of your Ringers adventure? We sure hope not! Go to one of your earlier choices and see what other possibilities await the gang.

"**L**ook, girls," said Willy. "It's not that we don't like you—as friends—or anything. It's just that football is something where you have to go all out."

"Yeah," Chris added. "And if you're playing, we'll have to hold back because we don't want to hurt you."

"And that won't be any fun," Willy continued. His eyes were warm and friendly. He was trying not to hurt the girls' feelings. "You understand?"

"Yeah," Sam piped up. "And if we're trying to impress you, we might get hurt ourselves." The other boys looked at him in surprise. Why would they want to impress the girls?

"Really," Sam went on, "I think it's better if just the guys play, OK?"

Jill looked sternly at each of the guys. Even Pete was nodding his head. She had to admit, she liked having these guys as friends—even if they were boys. But sometimes they could be so stubborn!

"Well, Tina," she said, with a shrug. "We'll just have to find our own adventure. Let's go down to the Freeze and get some ice cream." The two girls walked away briskly, not looking back.

Once they were out of earshot, Willy shouted, "All right! On to the Super Bowl! Last one to the field is a Dallas Cowboy!" The four boys went tearing down the street.

Meanwhile, the girls walked on to the center of town. They crossed Oak Street and looked in the window of the antique store. Tina loved the old furniture she saw there. There was something solid about it. They waited for the light to change and crossed Main Street. As they stepped into the grassy area of the town common, Jill suddenly sat down.

"Quick, Tina!" she cried. "Take off your shoes!"

In a moment, Tina was beside her, untying her sneakers and taking them off. "Why?" she asked. "What's wrong?"

Jill turned to her with a very serious look on her face. "This park has a special grass, imported from Tanzania in Africa. If it comes in contact with the rubber from your sneakers, it has a chemical reaction that gives off a special gas that can make you very sick."

"No!" Tina was staring at her friend in disbelief.

"And it pollutes the environment. But if you walk on this grass with bare feet, those same chemicals are good for you. They soak into your pores and into your blood stream, and they actually clean your blood. This grass even gives you better posture."

Tina had one eyebrow raised. She wasn't exactly buying this story, but Jill seemed so serious about this. And there was so much that Tina was still learning about America.

"I know it's hard to believe," Jill went on. "But it makes you healthier if you walk on this grass in bare feet. There were scientists here just last week collecting samples."

62

"I didn't see any—"

"They came at night. The dew makes the chemicals easier to collect."

"How do you know all this?"

"Betty told me." Betty Metz was the owner of the Freeze, the ice cream place just on the other side of the Common. She enjoyed kids and they loved her. "Come on," Jill said, leaping to her feet. "I'll show you."

Jill went scurrying across the Common in her bare feet, holding her shoes in one hand. Tina hurried after her. Jill went to one of the great oak trees that stood in the Common. She placed a hand on its bark and swung herself around it—and screamed.

 CHOICE

Turn to page 25.

The church had some stained-glass windows, but they were pretty dirty. Some were broken and boarded up. The result was an eerie glow in the sanctuary. The sun's rays seemed to slice the room, making some spots amber, some red, some blue. As they moved forward, Sam saw the strange colors playing on Pete's face. "Stop," he whispered. "You know, Pete, if you stayed right there all afternoon, you'd get a tie-dyed suntan."

Pete gave a sick smile. "You're weird, Ramirez."

The voice grew clearer. "I . . . waited . . . patiently," it said. "I . . . waited . . . patiently . . . for the Lord." It was coming from the office, just to the right of the sanctuary platform. The door was open, so the boys stepped in.

Mr. Whitehead was hunched over a small desk, his head in his hands. A Bible lay open on one side, a cup of coffee and bifocal glasses on the other.

"Uh, are you alright, Mr. Whitehead?" Pete asked timidly.

The old man was startled. "Who—who's that?" He looked up suddenly.

"I'm sorry, sir," said Pete. "We didn't mean to bother you. It looked like you were sick or something."

The man turned his warm eyes toward Pete. He smiled, but the boys could see there were tears on his cheeks. "No, Peter, I was just meditating on the Word."

"And the Bible makes you cry?" Sam felt bad about asking that as soon as the words left his mouth. But Mr. Whitehead didn't seem to mind.

"Sometimes," he answered. "I tell the Lord what a hard time I'm having, and he tells me to trust him. I don't always have as much faith as I should. And sometimes, I just feel old."

This was pretty astonishing. If a *retired missionary* didn't have enough faith, who did?

"What part of the Bible were you reading?" Pete asked.

The white-haired man reached with gentle hands to the Bible at his side. He fumbled with his glasses, put them on, and began to read.

"It's one of the Psalms, chapter 40. A Psalm of David—you remember, the kid who killed the giant."

The boys chuckled. There was a new spark in the man's eyes as he spoke now.

"It says, 'I waited patiently for the Lord.' Have you ever had to wait, boys? I mean really wait for something so long that you think it's never going to happen?"

"Yes," said Sam, thinking of his recent stay in the hole in the ground. "I can relate to that." He elbowed Pete in the ribs.

"Well, sometimes you even have to wait for the Lord," the minister continued. "'I waited patiently for the Lord; he turned to me and heard my cry. He lifted me out of the slimy pit, out of the mud and mire—'"

"Does it say that?" Sam jumped up with surprise. "Does it really say that?"

Mr. Whitehead turned the Bible so Sam could read it.

"Sure does. Have you ever felt like you were in a pit, surrounded by mud and mire?"

"Well, yes," Sam said, smiling. "As a matter of fact, I have. Have *you* ever felt like that, Mr. Whitehead?"

The old man leaned back in his chair. "Yes, my boys. Just today I was sitting here feeling sorry for myself. There's a lot of work involved in getting this church reopened. Sometimes I think it's never going to happen. I've been waiting for the Lord to send me some encouragement—some kind of a sign that I should keep going. I was really feeling like giving up. And then you two came along."

The boys were both surprised to find their eyes beginning to sting as they listened to the old man. Pete choked back his tears and said, "Please don't ever give up, Mr. Whitehead."

"Yeah," Sam added, "if you ever need our help, just let us know. We even have a secret for getting out of those miry pits—the Tallmaker."

Mr. Whitehead looked confused. "The tall-what?"

"Never mind."

And so it was that Sam, Pete, and Mr. Whitehead saved each other's day. Mr. Whitehead never forgot that moment in his office, and neither did the boys. It somehow encouraged them that someone like Mr. Whitehead could cry and need encouragement, too. Sam spent the next day writing out the first two verses of Psalm 40 and framing it. He gave it to Mr. Whitehead for Father's Day.

66

CHOICE ⇒

Of course, you still don't know how that "miry pit" got there, in the middle of Millersburg Common. Maybe if you retrace your steps to page 110 and make different choices, you'll find out.

Chris jumped up, ready to chase the kid, but Jill stopped him. "Maybe we should call the police."

"Who needs the police?" bellowed Chris. "I'll catch that kid in no time."

"Jill's right," said Betty from behind the counter. "Besides, how do you know that he took it?"

"Who else could have?" said Chris.

"Yeah," said Sam, "and what else would he have been doing here but getting into trouble? I saw him taking food off of people's plates."

"Well, yes," said Betty. "I saw him take some cookies from that booth over there, but the people had left, and I can't serve those cookies again anyway. I was going to offer him an ice cream cone, but he got scared and ran off."

"You were going to give him ice cream for free?" Jill asked.

"Sure. From the looks of him, I doubt he could afford to pay for it. Besides, he looked like he probably hadn't eaten all day."

"No," said Chris. "He probably stole a bunch of food."

"Yeah, let's call the police," said Sam.

Betty pulled a phone from under the counter. "Be my guest," she said. "But I don't think you should jump to conclusions. I mean, you don't have any proof that he took the ticket, do you? What do you think, Jim?"

Tina's eyes lit up. "Jim?"

Jim Whitehead, Tina's brother, stood up behind the counter, all smiles. He had been crouching there, waiting for the right moment.

"I thought you were at camp!" said Pete.

"I was," Jim replied. "But they gave me some time off for good behavior."

All the Ringers were up and crowding around Jim, welcoming him home. "Seriously, Jim," asked Pete, "what are you doing home?"

"Well, my grandfather wanted some help with a new idea he has. You see, he's really concerned about the homeless people in D.C. He wants to bring some of them out here, like for a week at a time, and give them some work to do, some good meals, a nice paycheck. You know, try to get them back on their feet."

It was dawning on everyone at the same time. "So that's who that kid was," said Sam.

"And that crazy woman in the Common," said Jill, with a glance toward Tina.

Chris was still bothered. "But isn't it dangerous to have them around here? I mean, that kid stole our ticket!"

"Are you sure about that?" said Jim, as he pulled the missing ticket from his shirt pocket.

"*You* had it!" screamed Jill.

"It was just a joke," said Jim. "I wanted to see how you'd react."

"How *did* we react?" said Sam quietly.

Jim thought for a moment. "Not too well. I can see my

grandfather and I have a lot of work to do, and it's not all among the homeless."

Over the next week, the Ringers got to know a number of homeless people—not only the little boy and the old woman (his grandmother), but his father and seven others. They all worked together to renovate the old church building.

And, as it turned out, they all went to the game. It was planned as a celebration for the beginning of Mr. Whitehead's homeless program. The Redskins office had donated a bunch of tickets. All ten homeless people went to the game, along with fifteen people from Millersburg—including all seven Ringers.

The Redskins won on a thrilling last-minute touchdown, a post-pattern pass from the quarterback to the rookie tight end Clyde Sterns. But the big thrill was that the whole group was invited to meet the players. Chris and Willy were in seventh heaven as they shook hands with their hero, Reggie Sanders. But Sam noticed how Deacon Joe Johnson took a special interest in the homeless people who were there. The hulking football player used his fame to make those people feel special.

Sam timidly asked Deacon Joe to sign his program. With a flourish, the Deacon wrote, "Joe Johnson, John 13:34-35."

"Wow!" Sam said, "Imagine putting a Bible verse after your name!" He could hardly wait to get home to look it up.

I don't care what the other guys say, Sam thought as he watched Deacon Joe talking with an old woman. *It*

70

takes more than a passing arm and good numbers to be a real hero.

Turn to page 124.

Chris was upset. The kid had gotten away, and now this woman was pestering him. What was she doing here anyway? This was a nice historic park in a nice suburban county; they didn't have "street people." Chris wished she would go away.

But she was still there. "Ya got a quarter? Sump'n to ee-eat?"

"No, I don't!" he snapped in his frustration, turning and stalking back into the Freeze.

The other Ringers didn't need to ask. The look on Chris's face told them that he had failed to catch the little thief.

"Are you sure he took it?" asked Betty from behind the counter.

"He was running all around there," said Sam. "Under the tables, under the counter stools. He's the only one who could have."

"Who is he, anyway?" asked Tina. Everyone shrugged.

"Never saw him before," said Willy.

Now they were left with three tickets—and four boys who wanted to go to the game. They agreed to flip a coin for it. Chris pulled a quarter from his pocket and called heads. Willy called tails. Jill flipped the coin—it came up tails. Then Pete called tails and lost to Sam. Then the two

72

losers—Pete and Chris—played. Chris called heads again, and moaned when the silver eagle showed up.

"Tails, Chris," said Jill. "I'm afraid you stay home with us."

"It's OK," said Chris. "You can see better on TV anyway."

As the three boys sat in the stadium before the game, along with Betty Metz and her husband, Pete had an idea.

"You know, the ticket that was stolen is for that seat there." He pointed to the empty seat next to Willy. "Whoever stole it will probably use it—so we'll find out who it was."

"Too late for Chris," Willy moaned.

"But what if the thief sold it?" suggested Sam.

Moments before kickoff, a well-dressed man in his mid-twenties came bounding up the stairs. He checked his ticket for the seat number and sat down next to Willy.

"I can't believe my luck today," he said to everyone around him. "At the last minute I decide to come to this game, see if I can get a ticket, right? And right out on the corner there's this old woman selling a single ticket. Ugliest woman I ever saw! But you know how much she charged me? A quarter. One little quarter. Can you believe that?"

The boys were only half listening, and none of them made the connection. Soon the game began.

THE END

Sam spoke first. "Come on, we're not the Redskins. We're just having fun." He stared down at the ground for a moment and then went on. "If the girls aren't playing, I guess I'm not playing either."

"Yeah, same here," said Pete. "And let's play touch, not tackle."

Everyone looked at Willy. He looked at his buddy Chris, then at Sam and Pete, then at the girls, then back at Chris. "Well, Chris," he said, "even if you are another Reggie Sanders, it ain't much of a game without those four. Come on, everyone! Last one to the apartment is a Philadelphia Eagle!"

Willy took off and was halfway down the block before the others realized what was happening. Chris shrugged and ran after him. Sam and Pete quickly followed.

"What's a Philadelphia Eagle?" Tina asked Jill.

"You don't want to know," Jill answered, as they both began running after the others.

Minutes later, they were all standing around in the field behind the apartment building where Willy's and Chris's families lived. "Where's Willy?" someone wondered out loud.

Just then they heard a crash from the garage. "Willy! Are you all right?" Tina shouted.

Before anyone could make a move toward the

garage, Willy came out the door, tossing a football, his black face beaming. "I can't believe how much junk we have in there," he laughed. Already, Chris was heading out for a pass. Willy lofted it high and long, right into Chris's hands—and right through them.

"Oops!" Chris called. "Maybe I'd better do the throwing."

The open field behind the apartment was just right for baseball in the summer and football in the fall—or, in this case, a rare game of late-summer football. There was a small, wooded area on the other side of the field. The boys had built a tree house in there when they were younger. And at one end of the field—in one "end zone"—was a ravine that sloped down to a small stream.

Chris and Willy chose up sides. Chris picked Pete and Tina. Willy had Sam and Jill. In spite of the heat, they were having fun.

Jill turned out to be a pretty good quarterback. Chris made fun of the way his cousin threw, but she got the ball to Willy and Sam. Soon her side was winning, two touchdowns to none. And they were about to score a third one.

The next play was Sam's idea. Willy ran five steps and turned around. Jill faked a throw to him. Chris, who was defending Willy, fell for it. He dove forward, but Willy was already running again, heading out toward the end zone. Jill easily lobbed the ball to him for another score.

Willy held the ball over his head as he trotted across the goal line. He looked back to tease Chris about the fake. "I got you this ti—"

Willy's bragging was cut short as he disappeared down the ravine.

All the others laughed, until they realized Willy wasn't coming back out. They ran to the end zone and looked into the ravine. Willy was holding his ankle and wincing with pain down by the stream.

Tina rushed to help him. "What happened?" she asked.

Embarrassed, Willy said, "Oh, nothing. I just twisted my ankle. I'll be all right." He struggled to get up. The other boys were there beside him, helping him stand.

"I don't think you should walk on that," said Tina. Willy insisted on climbing up the ravine and playing some more.

"Come on," he said, limping badly across the field. "It just hurts some. I'll be OK."

"Why don't you let my aunt look at it?" Tina asked. Her aunt was a nurse and worked at a doctor's office near the Metro station. "If we could get you to her clinic, I'm sure she could help."

Willy shook his head. "It's just a little pain. I can take it."

"Sure he can," Chris added. "Remember that game last year when Reggie Sanders played the last quarter with a busted rib? He was in pain something awful, but he won the game in the last minute."

"But you might hurt it worse if you keep playing," Jill protested. "Let's go see Tina's aunt. If your brother's home, Willy, maybe he can drive us."

"Oh, you girls don't know anything," Chris shouted.

76

"This is a tough sport. We guys are used to playing with pain. And Willy's as tough as they come."

At that moment, Willy didn't look so sure.

CHOICE

If Willy keeps playing, turn to page 112.

If Willy goes to see Tina's aunt, turn to page 118.

Betty overheard the girls' whispers as she wiped the counter. "Why not tell them?" she said loudly. "They're going to find out soon enough."

Jill paused to look at the four boys. A plan was already forming in her mind. "I guess you're right," she agreed. Then she announced to the boys that she and Tina had four very special tickets, and it was up to them to decide who would use them.

"Tickets?" Chris blurted out. "To what?"

"Probably to the flower show or something," Willy said. The boys all snickered.

"No," Jill said firmly. "These are tickets that you would all *love* to have. But there are only four, so we can't all go."

"Go where?" Chris asked, a bit louder.

The others were joining in. "Yeah, Jill, quit teasing. What are they for?"

Jill flashed an impish smile at Tina. "Oh, just a Redskins game."

"You're lying," said Chris. "It's not even football season yet."

Willy put his hand on Chris's shoulder. *"Pre*season, buddy. They have their first game next Saturday." He turned back to Jill. "Is that the game?" he asked. She nodded.

"ALL RIGHT!!" Willy shouted, putting his fist high into the air. "I've never been to a Redskins game before!"

"Me, neither!" yelled Chris, raising his hands for a set of high fives with Willy. "We are going to have a blast!"

Sam was the only one not smiling. "What do you mean, 'we', Kimosabe?" Suddenly the room was quiet. In one booth, a mother and young daughter were finishing an afternoon sundae. In a back booth, a high school senior and his girlfriend were gazing at each other over melting ice cream. The door clanged open briefly, and a small boy scurried inside.

Of course, none of the Ringers took much notice of any of this. They were all staring at Sam, waiting for him to explain. Sam milked the moment for all it was worth. He loved attention.

Then Pete broke the silence. "Keemo-sabee?"

"It's Redskin talk," Sam muttered. "You know, Lone Ranger and Tonto?"

Pete turned to the others and shrugged. "Too many reruns," he explained. "Brain damage."

"No, really," Sam went on. "Jill said she only has four tickets, remember? We don't know who's using them. Right, Jill?"

"Very good, Sam," Jill answered. "You know, you're not as dumb as you look."

"Thanks . . . I think."

To everyone's surprise, Tina interrupted. The normally shy girl explained that Betty had given them the tickets and suggested that they invite Chris and Jim. But Jim was off at camp and—

"That's OK," Willy jumped in. "I'll take his ticket."

Jill just shook her head. She was enjoying this. "But you boys haven't been very nice to us lately. I don't know why we should give you anything."

The boys pleaded their case. They were just joking around, they said. They didn't mean anything. They didn't play football anyway.

"As I see it," Jill continued, "there are two things we could do. One, we could choose the two nicest boys and let them go to the game with us—"

Tina suddenly seemed upset. "Not *with us,*" she interrupted. "Just at the same time. I mean, it's not a date or anything."

Everyone looked horrified at the thought. "No. No way. Not at all. Yuk!"

"What's the second choice?" Sam asked.

"Well, I'd need to talk this over with Tina, but we could just give you the four tickets, in exchange for some special favor."

"Like what?" asked Chris, suspiciously.

"Like maybe you have to promise to include us in everything you do from now on."

"Forever?" Willy gasped.

Jill thought for a moment and said, "Well, let's say for the next year."

Chris was quiet for a minute. "I think we could do that," he finally said.

Jill and Tina retreated to the counter stools to make their decision. "I don't know," said Tina. "Maybe we should just give them the tickets. I'm not that crazy about football anyway."

"But we have to get something in return," Jill protested.

"Why? Can't we just be nice?"

"They haven't been very nice to us!"

"Well," Tina said quietly, "my great-aunt Millie always used to say, 'It's up to me to start the niceness.'"

CHOICE ➡

If the girls decide to just give the tickets to the boys, turn to page 32.

If the girls choose the two nicest boys to go with them (*at the same time!*) to the game, turn to page 10.

Sam grabbed the closest thing he could find and bellowed to the dim shape in the darkness, "Don't come any closer. I have a ketchup bottle."

He heard that high-pitched squeak again—the creature—but it sounded like words. It sounded like, "Don't hurt me!"

"Don't hurt *you?*" Sam hollered back. "Don't you hurt *me!*"

"I won't," squeaked the creature in the darkness. "I promise."

"Come out here where I can see you," Sam ordered.

"Put my bottle down," answered the voice.

"Your bottle?"

"That's all my stuff."

Sam was still holding the bottle high, like a club. He didn't want to take any chances. "So are you coming out?" he asked, impatiently.

"How do I know you won't hurt me?" the voice responded.

Sam was frustrated. "Well, how do I know you won't hurt *me?*"

There was silence. Neither of them moved. It was a standoff. Suddenly Sam had an idea.

"If you don't come out here by the time I count to fifteen, I'm going to take all your stuff here and run through that tunnel." He was hoping the tunnel led somewhere.

The creature let out a long, pained whimper. "Don't!!"

"One," Sam said firmly. "Two, three . . ."

There was a ruffle of movement.

"Six, seven, eight . . ."

The dim shape was getting clearer in the light that danced from the candle in the corner.

"Thirteen, fourteen . . ."

Sam froze in surprise.

A young boy stepped into the alcove. Sam guessed he was seven or eight. His face was filthy, his hair was tangled, and he smelled bad. His eyes looked this way and that, never resting.

"Put down my bottle," the boy said sternly.

Sam had forgotten that the ketchup bottle was still in his upraised hand. He brought it down slowly. "What's your name?"

"Everyone calls me Sonny," the boy squeaked.

"I'm Sam. Pleased to meet you." Sam started to reach out for a handshake, but when he saw how dirty the boy was, he decided not to.

"What are you doing here?" Sonny asked suspiciously.

"I–I fell into that hole," Sam stammered. "I didn't know what to do. I crawled down here. Then you scared me."

"*I* scared *you?*"

"When you lit that match. I didn't know what you were."

The boy's darting eyes looked down sadly. "What am I?" he asked.

"Well," Sam answered, "you're a person. A kid. I can see that now. But I couldn't see that in the dark."

"You just came to take my stuff." Sonny lurched forward and began to gather the bag and the can in his grimy hands.

"No, I didn't!" Sam protested. "I don't care about your st—"

All of a sudden Sam realized he was apologizing to a seven-year-old about stumbling onto his private collection of trash. There was something strange about all this.

"Wait a second," Sam demanded. "Where do you live?"

The boys eyes darted more wildly this time. "Around," he said.

"Where? On Oak Street? Maple? How come I haven't seen you around before?"

"I've seen *you,*" the boy snapped.

"Where? Where have you seen me?"

"In the ice cream place," Sonny answered. "With your friends."

The memory flickered through his mind. It was just an hour ago or less, but it seemed like years. Sam remembered wondering what that little kid had been doing in the Freeze, but then the group had been sidetracked on other things.

"That's where you got the tickets!" Sam charged. Sonny scurried to grab the small white envelope with the four football tickets sticking out, but Sam grabbed it first.

"You little sneak! How could you steal these tickets from the girls? These are valuable."

"I didn't steal them. They're mine."

"Right. Where's a little kid like you going to get tickets to a Redskins game?"

"A man gave them to us. Honest. They're for me and my father and Gram and the Reverend."

That still sounded fishy to Sam. "Gram" and "The Reverend"? Sounded like tag-team wrestling.

The boy was back to his high-pitched whine. "Give me back my tickets."

Sam held them away from Sonny. "I still don't think they're yours."

"But they are! They're for me and my father and—"

"And Gram and the Reverend. I know, I know." Sam nodded, humoring the boy. "Just who is this 'Gram'?"

"My Gramma. She's old and sick, but the Reverend thinks he can get help for her."

"What does this Reverend look like?" Sam was beginning to buy this story.

"His hair's all white. He's pretty old, too. At least forty. And he has a real nice face. I like his face. I don't like yours."

Well, thanks, Sam thought. *You're not exactly Emilio Estevez yourself, kid.* But he didn't say this. He kept grilling the boy.

"What's this Reverend's name?"

"I don't know," Sonny said. Then his face showed remembrance. "Mr. Whitehair. That's it!"

Sam gave a knowing smile. "And if we go to

Reverend 'Whitehair' and ask him about the tickets, he'll back you up?"

"He should," Sonny chirped. "It's the truth."

Sam had a plan. He grabbed a piece of twine that was sitting among Sonny's "stuff" and had the boy tie it around his leg. "I want to be sure you don't crawl away from me in the tunnel," he said. "Now we're going to see the Reverend."

Turn to page 102.

In a flash, Chris was up and running out the door. "I'll get you, you little thief!"

He saw the boy running across the Common, toward the church. The kid was halfway across the grassy park, but Chris figured he could catch him. *I'm another Reggie Sanders,* he thought. *I pass, I run, I uphold the law.*

Chris reached full speed in ten strides and was clearly gaining on the little thief. Then the boy disappeared. He just wasn't there anymore. Chris blinked a few times, hoping he didn't need glasses. He slowed to a trot and scanned the area. The boy was nowhere to be found.

Maybe he veered off into those trees when I wasn't looking, Chris thought. He went to his right, where a couple of oak trees loomed. Nothing there. He circled back toward the Freeze, wondering how he would explain this to his friends.

As he passed another tree, the big maple directly across from the Freeze, he heard a sound. It was just a shuffling of feet, but Chris knew he had his man. He moved extra slowly around the tree, ready to nab his suspect. He caught a glimpse of a sneaker, so he pounced . . . and came face-to-face with the ugliest woman he had ever seen.

She was old, with wrinkles all over her face. Most of her teeth were missing, and the ones she had were bad.

Her clothes were old and dirty. She carried an oversized pocketbook. And, of course, she wore sneakers.

It looked as if she had been sleeping on her feet. Chris's pouncing had not fazed her at all. Chris, on the other hand, thought his heart was going to pound through his chest. The woman "woke up" and said calmly, as she had a million times before, "Ya got a quarter, sir? Sump'n to ee-eat?"

"Uh, no . . . I'm, uh, I'm looking for somebody," Chris said nervously. "A little boy, about this tall. Have you seen him?"

The woman chuckled a little. "Heh, heh, heh. That Sonny. You'll never catch him. Ya got a quarter? You help me, I help you. Sump'n to ee-eat?"

There was a music to the way she said it. It was her rap. She had obviously practiced it on many street corners.Chris almost felt sorry for her, but he had to catch the little crook.

"Can you tell me where the boy went?" he asked urgently.

"Heh, heh, heh. That Sonny. You'll never catch him. Ya got a quarter?"

CHOICE ⟾

If Chris gives the woman a quarter, turn to page 18.

If Chris does not give the woman anything, turn to page 71.

Jill and Chris didn't talk much over the next week and a half. Chris was spending a lot of time at Willy's place, helping to keep Willy from being bored out of his mind.

As for Jill, she still felt guilty. But she told herself that she deserved the ticket more than Chris did. After all, Chris had been mean to her and tried to keep the girls from playing football. Sure, he had stayed with Willy instead of going to the Freeze, but maybe he was just tired of being with the others.

She only half believed all this, but she kept on acting as if she really did believe it—right through to Saturday night. She sat at the game with Tina, Sam, Pete, and Betty and her husband. She tried to enjoy the game, but she kept thinking about Chris. He had been a good friend to Willy, staying with him when he needed help—even when there was a surprise promised at the Freeze. "Why can't I be as good a friend to him?" Jill asked herself.

Everyone else went to Willy's house afterward for a victory party, but Jill couldn't face her cousin that night. She asked to be dropped off at home. It was another three days before Jill straightened things out with Chris. She offered a stuttering apology. Chris wasn't sure what she was apologizing for, but he accepted it anyway. Girls are like that sometimes, he figured—hard to understand.

THE END

"**N**ever could resist a mystery, huh?" gasped Chris as they kept running.

"Nope," answered Willy. "Let's find that kid."

They turned a corner and saw the boy at the end of the hallway. He was frantically pulling on a locked door. Then he tried the door across from it. It wouldn't budge. He was trapped.

He turned to face Chris and Willy and seemed pleased to find that his pursuers were only a few years older than he was. "Who are you?" he asked.

"Who are *you?*" Chris countered.

"I asked you first," said the boy.

Just then they heard voices and footsteps behind them. The men were catching up.

"Quick!" said Willy. "Chris, go through there." He pointed to a narrow metal door in the wall.

"You're kidding," said Chris.

"No, it'll be fun. It's a laundry chute. Just land on your feet. I'll give you five seconds, then I'll send the kid down. When he hits bottom, hang onto him."

Chris climbed through the opening and slid down the chute, landing in a bin of dirty clothes. He quickly moved out of the way. The boy came tumbling down after him. Just as the men turned the corner, Willy went sliding down the chute himself. He hoped there were enough towels at the bottom to keep his ankle from getting hurt again. His soft landing was a relief.

Safely in the basement, Chris and Willy dragged the boy to a corner and started grilling him with questions. For every question they asked, the boy asked one in return.

"This is getting us nowhere," Chris complained. "Look, we'll do it this way. One of us will ask a question. Then I will answer for myself, you will answer for yourself, and Willy will answer for himself. All right?"

The boy nodded.

"First," Chris continued, "who are you and where are you from?"

"That's two questions."

Chris ignored that. "I'm Chris Martin from Millersburg."

Reluctantly, the boy said, "I'm Joey Wright from D.C."

"And I'm Willy Washington from Millersburg."

"Good," Chris went on. "Second question: What are you doing here? *I'm* just trying to watch my favorite football team."

"Me too," said Joey.

Willy grabbed his shirt threateningly. "More specific information!"

The boy cracked. "All right! My dad is a sports reporter for the *Post*. This practice is closed to the press, but Pop wanted to get a story anyway. So he thought I could sneak in.And I did."

"How?" Willy asked.

"Through the air vents. Don't ever try it," he said, rubbing his shins. "It hurts."

"So have you gotten your story yet?" asked Chris.

"Well, I haven't been out to the field yet. But, as I was sneaking past one of the offices, I heard these men talking about stolen tickets. I figured that might be a bigger story, so I kept listening—until I fell out."

The boy told Chris and Willy what he heard. Five thousand tickets were going to be handed out free all over D.C. and the surrounding suburbs. The team's public relations director had had them in his briefcase, which was left in Coach Winston's office. Somebody had broken in and stolen the tickets.

"Would you like to know who that 'somebody' was?" Willy asked. "I may have a scoop for you." He told Joey all about the conversation they had overheard between Greg and his girlfriend.

Joey was overjoyed with this tip. "I need a phone and directions to Greg's office," he said. With Willy's help, he called the coach's office and anonymously told him where to find the tickets. Then he hid out next to Greg's office, waiting until the coach came (with two security guards) to get the tickets back.

The story was in the paper the next day. Willy recognized some of his own quotes, credited to "an informed source." He cut out the article for his scrapbook—just one more memento of a fabulous summer.

THE END

This isn't the only ending. Have you fallen into Sam's pit yet? If not, turn back to page 34 and make other choices.

"I just think it should be our little secret," said Jill, loud enough for the boys to hear.

Tina wasn't so sure. "But what about—?"

Jill broke in quickly. "What about the 'extras'? Well, we've got some time to figure that out."

The boys were dying of curiosity, but they were trying to play it cool. Suddenly Sam said, "Oh girls, you'll never guess what we found out on the way over here!"

The other boys were giving Sam strange looks, but Jill didn't notice. "What?" she asked.

"Can't tell you." Sam grinned at her. "It's a secret."

Tina piped up: "Well, if it's about the special grass from Africa that's in the Common, we already know that."

"What special grass?" Pete asked with a smirk.

"You know—the grass that gives off a special gas if you have sneakers on."

"Oh, that," Sam said with a straight face. "The gas grass."

The other boys were busting their guts trying not to laugh. Even Jill, who felt bad about telling Tina that story, was having a hard time hiding a smile.

Tina kept going: "I walked on it in my bare feet, like you're supposed to. And, you know, my posture already feels better."

"Posture?" Chris asked.

"Oh yes," Sam assured. "Pete has been walking barefoot in it all his life. That's why he's so tall. Right, Pete?"

Pete was beginning to feel bad for Tina. He raised his right hand and said, "I cannot tell a lie. This whole thing is—" but Tina interrupted him.

"And I would never have known any of this if it weren't for Jill."

"Aha!" said Chris. "So *Jill* told you all of this." Jill looked down, embarrassed.

"Tina," Pete blurted out, "it's not true. Any of it. It's just a story. Jill was—we all were—having fun with you."

Tina looked slowly around the group. "I knew that," she said with false confidence. Then she excused herself and went to the ladies room.

"So," Chris asked Jill. "Are you going to tell us your secret now, or what?"

"Or what," Jill replied, smiling sweetly. She was enjoying this entirely too much. She stepped proudly over to the counter to ask Betty for a glass of water. The four boys put their heads together.

"I don't like this. Let's get out of here."

"No, I think we can get Tina to spill the beans."

"Forget it. Let's just get some ice cream."

"No, let's just leave. We can go play football."

"Too hot."

"We could go over to my place and play video games."

"Nah, I don't want to leave."

Then Jill and Tina were both back at the booth.

CHOICE ⇒

If the boys decide to leave, turn to page 105.

If the boys decide to try to get Tina to tell them the secret, turn to page 57.

The boys took off around the stadium. The guards began to chase them. Willy was favoring his injured ankle. He definitely wasn't in top form.

"If we get around to the hole in the fence, we can sneak through and hide," Willy panted.

"Just keep moving," Chris urged.

The guards seemed to be gaining slightly as the boys turned the corner of the stadium. They were now on the end zone side. If they could only find the place to sneak through.

"I can't find it!" said Chris in a panic.

"Be cool," said Willy, as his eyes searched the fenceposts he was passing. Sure enough, he found a red marking on one of the metal struts. "Here it is!"

The beauty of this entryway was that the hole was not directly under the fence. That's why it had never been discovered by the authorities and filled in. The hole was a foot inside the fence. But you could push the chain-link fencing forward enough to slide under, into the hole.

Willy and Chris quickly did just that and looked for a place to hide. An old tarp was lying nearby. "Follow me!" whispered Willy as he rushed over to the tarp. He pulled it over them both as the guards came around the corner.

Peeking from their hiding place, they saw the guards'

feet as they paced back and forth outside the fence. "They vanished!" one said.

"Probably ran into the woods," said the other.

"At least they didn't get in."

"Kids! I've had enough of 'em for one day."

The feet strolled away.

Now the boys heard only those grunts.

UH-uh-uh-uh-UH-uh-uh-uh. A minute later, Willy lifted the tarp and stepped out. On the field below, the Redskins players were doing exercises.

"There they are," gasped Willy.

"In real life," Chris whispered in awe.

"Someone will find us here," Willy said quietly. "Let's run over to the stands."

Willy knew his way around this place. Zeke used to work as a ball boy for some of the college teams, and he used to bring Willy around sometimes. When Zeke was working with the teams, little Willy would wander. He knew all the stadium's passageways.

Going through an unmarked door, the boys entered a dimly lit hallway. Along one side were several offices. "The food managers work here," Willy whispered. "You know, the ones who sell refreshments. They're usually only here on weekends."

Walking down the hall, they were surprised to hear voices in one of the offices—one male, one female.

"Five thousand of them, Sandy! Think what we can do with five thousand!"

"But how can you sell them?"

"I've got connections. A few phone calls is all it takes."

Chris and Willy were crouching beneath the office windows. "I know them," said Willy. "That's Greg and his girlfriend. Greg sells candy at the college games."

"It's a big game, honey," Greg went on. "I figure we could clear twenty bucks on each one."

"Twenty bucks?"

"This ain't peanuts, honey. Or Cracker Jack."

"But that would be . . . what, ten thousand dollars?"

"A hundred! A hundred grand!"

"Wow! Maybe then we could get married."

"Sure, hon. I told you. Stick with me and I'll make you rich."

Willy was pulling at Chris's arm. "Let's get out of here." They scurried through the hallway to another unmarked door.

Turn to page 38.

Sam couldn't believe it. "Tina? Tina's the one who passes?"

"No, not Tina," Pete said with a smirk. "But who *is* the one who *passes?*"

"The quarterback," said Tina. "Even I know that!"

Jill nodded with understanding. "That was a pretty good one."

"Reminds me of this story about a coach who was trying to get a team together," said Sam. "He went to this pay phone to call this wide receiver he knew. He put in his quarter and dialed the number, and it was busy. He dialed again and it was busy. He dialed again and again. Always busy. Do you think he ever got his wide receiver?"

"No," said Pete. "But I hope he at least got his *quarter back.*"

"Oh, you heard it before," Sam protested.

Pete denied it. "I could see it coming a mile away."

To everyone's surprise, Tina piped up again: "So I guess the receiver was off the hook."

Catching the mood, Jill added, "You just couldn't *pass* that one up, could you?"

Just then Betty came back, wiping her hands. "So, did you solve my riddle?"

"We think so," said Pete. "It was the quarterback who 'passed'."

"Right you are," Betty remarked with a flourish. "And for that correct answer you win four free tickets to the Washington Redskins game next Saturday!"

"You're kidding!" Their mouths dropped open in surprise.

"Early this morning," Betty continued, "just before you came in, Pete, a man came by offering free tickets. He gave me six. My husband and I will use two, and that leaves four for you. It works out perfectly."

"Thank you," they were all saying. "That's really nice of you, Betty."

Meanwhile, Chris and Willy were hanging out in Willy's living room watching TV when the phone rang.

"Don't move," Chris said. "I've got it."

It was Willy's mom. "Who is this?" she asked suspiciously.

"It's me, Chris."

"I sure hope Willy is paying you enough to answer our phone for him. Is he there?"

"Well, yes, but he's kind of hurting right now. You see, we were playing football, and he kind of twisted his ankle."

"Is it serious?"

"Well, Mrs. Washington, Willy probably doesn't want me to say this, but I think it is. I'm kind of worried."

"I'll be right there."

Willy was able to see the doctor that night. He learned that he'd be out of action for at least a week. The doctor scolded him for continuing to play on the ankle. That had made it worse.

Back at the Freeze, the four ticketholders were splurging on ice cream sodas, celebrating their good fortune. But Jill was getting quieter and quieter.

"What's wrong?" Tina finally asked.

"I just keep thinking about Chris and Willy. They would love to go to this game. Shouldn't we give them our tickets?"

Sam replied quickly, "Just because something good happens to us doesn't mean we have to feel guilty. We were in the right place at the right time. They could have come with us."

"Come on," Jill barked back. "Willy wasn't going anywhere. And Chris was right to stay with him. Somebody had to."

"Look, Willy decided to keep playing on that bad ankle," Pete observed. "If he didn't, he'd probably be here with us. And, as I recall, it was Chris who talked him into it. They deserve to be left out."

Jill wasn't agreeing. "No one deserves to be left out," she mumbled. "I just wish we had two more tickets."

The conversation stalled with no decision being made. One by one the gang filtered out, and everyone went home.

CHOICE ⇒

If Jill decides to give Chris her ticket, turn to page 15.

If Jill decides to keep her ticket for herself, turn to page 88.

Suddenly Sam remembered his problem. "How are we going to climb out of the hole?"

"What hole?" the boy asked, innocently.

"The hole I fell into, stupid."

"I don't know anything about a hole, *stupid!*" The boy's extra emphasis made Sam feel—well, stupid. Sonny pointed to the other tunnel, Sam's planned escape route. "That should take us right to the church."

Sonny crawled confidently through this other passageway, with Sam following, holding the rope. Then Sonny pushed aside a piece of plywood, and they barreled through an opening into a room. This looked familiar to Sam. They *were* under the church. He had explored these secret tunnels with the Ringers, but they must have missed this particular one.

The two made their way up to the sanctuary of the old church. Sam noticed an old woman sitting in the front pew. The boy ran right up to her, put his arms around her, and said, "Hi, Gram!" Her face was very wrinkled. She had few teeth. And she seemed to be staring into space. But her face did brighten a bit when Sonny hugged her.

Then Sonny bounced through the door into the church office. Sam, still holding the rope, was yanked in behind him. Mr. Whitehead was talking with a man whom Sam had never seen before. He had a scraggly beard and his clothes were old, but his eyes were bright and he smiled a lot. Sonny crawled into his lap, saying, "Hi, Pop!"

"Well, Sam," said Mr. Whitehead, who didn't seem to mind the interruption. "I see you've found a new friend."

Sonny was suddenly talking a mile a minute. "Sam-doesn't-believe-that-man-gave-us-the-tickets-and-that-they're-really-ours-he-thinks-I-stoled-them-tell-him-it's-true-we're-still-going-to-the-game-aren't-we?"

"Yes, of course." Mr. Whitehead smiled then looked at Sam. "You see, Sam, Sonny's father, Mr. Worth, is going to do some work for us around the church, fixing things up and getting things ready. He's been without a job for—how long? A couple of years?"

Mr. Worth nodded. "Too long," he said.

"And he and his mother and his son have been trying to survive on the streets for a while. So we figured we'd bring them out here and give them a chance."

"Tell him about the tickets!" Sonny begged.

"Oh, that was a surprise," Mr. Whitehead explained. "This morning a man came by the church and offered us these free tickets. So I'm going to take these three fine people to the game next week. I sent the man over to the Freeze to try to catch up with you kids. Didn't you see him?"

They talked a bit more that day. Later, Gram decided not to go to the game, so the Worths offered Sam the extra ticket. Sam's day turned out all right after all.

As Sam left the church that afternoon, Mr. Worth asked, "So tell me, how did you boys meet?"

104

Sam smiled at Sonny before answering, "Oh, I sort of dropped in on him."

If you haven't been to the game with the Ringers yet, turn to page 34 and make different choices.

"We're leaving," said Chris, getting up from the booth. The others slid out as well.

"Why?" asked Tina. "What's wrong?"

As Chris spoke, his eyes shot daggers at Jill. "Well, obviously you have some secrets you don't want to share with us. So we have no reason to stick around. See ya."

Jill was upset. "You should talk! Who wouldn't let us play football, huh? You weren't exactly jumping at the chance to share with us!"

"Well, that's different—," Willy started to say.

Jill cut him off. "But if that's the way you're going to be, we're never going to share anything with you again."

"Fine!" shouted Chris on his way out.

It was a miserable three days before the boys and girls did anything together again. It was a week before Chris and Jill finally spoke to each other again. When they did, they realized how silly it all was, and they forgave each other.

Unfortunately, it was too late to do anything about the tickets.

THE END

Chris saw a side door and went through it. "Forget him," he said, as he pulled Willy through. They were in a room with several chairs set up. It looked like it could be a team meeting room.

"Where are we now?" asked Chris.

"I don't know," Willy answered. "I got lost on that last turn."

Across the room was a door leading to another hallway. They heard voices, and suddenly two big men in football gear walked by.

"That was Reggie!" Chris gasped.

"No!"

"I'd know him anywhere! That was him!"

They hurried across the room and peeked out the door.

"It's number 8! Sanders! What did I tell you?"

"Now's your chance, Chris. Go get his autograph."

"I couldn't!"

"It's now or never."

"But I don't have any paper."

Willy pulled a pack of football cards from Chris's back pocket. There was Reggie Sanders at the top of the pile. "Try this," Willy said.

Timidly, Chris took the card and ventured down the hall. Willy was a few paces behind. Chris turned a corner and there was his hero, not five feet away. Sanders had stopped and was talking heatedly with another player. His language was filled with profanity. "I don't give a ——— what anybody thinks! I'll show up when I feel like showing up! I know how much practice I need! I'm the star of this ——— team! I've got the big contract, OK? What are they going to do, fire me?"

"Excuse me, Mr. Sanders," Chris said softly. His voice sounded small and girlish. He tried to deepen it. "EXCUSE ME, MR. SANDERS. COULD I HAVE YOUR AUTOGRAPH?"

Just as Willy came around the corner behind Chris, he saw Reggie Sanders give Chris a disgusted look. "Get lost, kid! Who let these kids in here anyway? I thought this was a closed practice! I hate kids. Get 'em out of here!"

As Sanders walked away, Chris stood there stunned, trying to hold back the tears. He still held the Reggie Sanders card in his outstretched hand. As he watched his idol go, Chris slowly ripped the card in half and let the pieces fall to the floor.

"Come on, Chris," Willy said. "Let's go home." He put his arm around Chris's shoulder and turned him around.

Just then, a huge, padded body turned the corner and knocked the two boys down. Willy and Chris went sprawling, one to the right, the other to the left. A big, black man leaned down with real concern showing on his face. "I'm so sorry, guys. I didn't see you there. Are you OK?"

They were fine, just surprised. They looked up . . . and up . . . and up. The guy was huge! It was Deacon Joe Johnson.

"Hey, listen. I wasn't watching where I was going. Will you forgive me?"

"Sure, Joe," said Willy.

A smile broke across Chris's face.

"Have you been crying, my man?" the Deacon asked. "Did I do that to you?"

"No," Chris sighed. "It was Reggie."

The Deacon nodded knowingly. "That boy has a lot to learn."

"Boy?" Willy asked.

"Oh, sure," Johnson answered. "When I was Reggie's age, he was your age. In fact, he tells me he once asked for my autograph."

"Did you give it to him?" Chris wondered.

"Of course. Every football player owes his career to boys like you. We can't afford to forget that." Deacon Joe let out a long, low sigh. "Unfortunately, Reggie often does forget. But I've been prayin' for him. Maybe if you pray, too, God will work a miracle in his heart."

Willy was surprised. "You pray?"

"Of course." Joe grinned. That's why they call me 'the Deacon'! Hey, I gotta get out there if I want to make this team."

He stood up to his full stature and started down the hall. Chris pulled a card out of Willy's shirt pocket and hurried after him. "Oh, Joe. Could you sign this for me?"

"You bet, champ," he said, looking over the football card and taking the pen Chris handed him. "I didn't know they were still making cards of me. What's your name, son?"

And so it was that Chris and Willy met Deacon Joe Johnson.

Ever since that day, Chris kept that card in his special drawer. Whenever he looks at it, it reminds him of that crazy summer with the Ringers. Every so often he takes it out and rereads the flowing handwriting: "Chris, keep praying. Keep trusting. Keep loving. John 13:34-35."

THE END

Pretty neat to get to meet players like that, huh? If you haven't read what other neat adventures await Chris and Willy, turn back to page 34 and make other choices. Or turn to page 124.

"Embarrassed?" Sam shouted. "Why would I be embarrassed? Just because I can't cross the Common without running into a tree and falling into a hole—"

"What tree?"

"Don't ask. Just find someone with a rope or ladder and get me out of here."

Pete stopped reaching. "Yeah, I guess that's the best thing. I'll get some help." He stood up and dusted himself off. Leaning over the hole, he said, "Now you stay there." Then he left.

"Stay here?" Sam grunted. "Right. Like I have a choice." Then he waited. The minutes dragged on. Suddenly he heard a voice, not from above, but to the side. He was expecting to hear Pete approaching at the top of the pit. Instead, he heard a strange voice in the distance.

He reached in that direction, expecting to touch a cold dirt wall. There was nothing. He took a step in that direction, with his hands out in front of him. Still nothing. After another step, he was in darkness. The blue sky was not above him anymore. He was in an underground passageway leading away from the pit!

Sam's curiosity rose five notches. Where did this lead? Maybe under the bank on Oak Street. Maybe some robbers were planning a heist. Or maybe this led under the Freeze, and some teenage pranksters were planning to raid the ice-cream supplies. Maybe it was left over from the days of the Underground Railroad, a secret escape route for runaway slaves. Maybe it hooked up with the tunnels in the church basement. Or maybe these were just old sewer lines.

Should he follow the passageway? Or should he stay put? Pete would probably be back any minute with rope or a ladder. But Pete had been gone a long time, it seemed. Maybe he forgot. Maybe he went back to the Freeze and started arguing with the others.

What would Sam find in this passageway? Buried treasure? Giant alligators? He was excited and scared at the same time. But wouldn't it be cool to have a secret hideout here, where he could just vanish from the others?

CHOICE

If Sam investigates the passageway, turn to page 7.

If Sam stays put, turn to page 121.

"**C**ome on, Willy," Chris prodded. "You're not going to wimp out on us, are you?"

Willy hobbled over to pick up the football. "No, I'll be fine," he said. "Let's play some ball."

With that, he fired the ball to Chris. "OK," Chris said, "you guys kick off."

They went back to the game, but it wasn't as much fun. The girls were especially worried about Willy's ankle. And even Chris eased up a bit when he was playing against him.

Still, Chris's team managed to score three touchdowns in a short time. Pete could easily outrun Willy now, and he caught every one of Chris's spiraling passes.

Everyone noticed that Willy seemed to be hurting a bit more on each play. After the third touchdown, Chris said, "Hey, let's call it. I'm gettin' tired."

The others seemed relieved. "Three to three," said Jill. "I'd say that's pretty even."

"Hey, Willy," yelled Sam from across the field. "You got anything cold to drink inside?"

Willy didn't answer at first.

"Hey, Willy," Chris added, slapping his friend on the back, "you gonna invite us in?"

"Uh, yeah," Willy answered. "Yeah, let's go in." He seemed to be out of it. Chris kept his arm around Willy and sensed that Willy was leaning hard on him, favoring that ankle.

Willy sat down as soon as he got inside. It was Chris who got iced tea for everyone. They sat around and talked about sports and camp and food and the weather—anything but Willy's ankle.

"Oh, I almost forgot," Pete said suddenly. "I was at the Freeze this morning, and Betty said we should all come over later. She has a surprise for us."

They all seemed excited about it. The conversation was winding down anyway, so they got up to go—all but Willy and Chris. "Come on, Willy," said Pete. "You gonna join us?"

"I don't think so," Willy answered. He propped up his throbbing ankle and vowed not to move.

"What about you, Chris?"

"I don't know," Chris answered, with a glance toward Willy. "Maybe I'd better stay here."

"Go ahead if you want," Willy urged. But Chris could tell that Willy really wanted him to stay.

CHOICE ⇒

If Chris goes with the gang, turn to page 29.

If Chris stays with Willy, turn to page 5.

"**E**mbarrass me?" Sam asked. "What do you mean by that?"

Pete stretched his long arm farther down toward Sam. "I don't know. I just think it wouldn't be too cool for me to run back to the Freeze and say, 'Hey, everybody! Sam fell into a hole!' How did you do that anyway?"

"It was easy," Sam cracked. "I just went down. Now just reach a little farther—I can almost touch your fingertips."

Pete tried to dig the toes of his sneakers into the turf. Then he lowered his whole upper body into the hole. Passersby glanced over as they walked along the street. They saw only a pair of legs sticking out of the ground.

Inside the pit, Sam could now reach Pete's arms. "Grab my wrists with your hands," Pete grunted, "and I'll grab yours."

Sam did exactly that. Clinging to Pete's wrists, he tried to pull himself up. "Hold it," gasped Pete. "I think I'm slip-p-p-p—"

Pete's toes lost their grip. The lanky boy slipped headfirst into the hole. At the edge of the park, the aged Mr. Weatherly was taking his daily stroll. From a distance, he saw Pete's legs lose their toehold, shoot up in the air, and sink straight down. It reminded him of the sinking of some great ship on the ocean. "Fire torpedoes!" he said with a cackle.

"Are you OK?" Sam asked his upside-down friend.

"Yeah, I'm fine. It's only my head."

"Right," Sam laughed. "Hard as steel."

"Actually, I broke the fall with my arms," Pete explained.

"And my foot."

"Oh, did I land on your foot?"

"It's all right. I have another one."

There was a strained laugh, then silence. Finally Pete said, "Uh, Sam. Do you think I could turn right-side-up now?"

"Be my guest."

It was easier said than done, however. In the cramped area of the pit, the next few minutes were a confusion of arms and legs.

"Turn that way."

"This way?"

"No, that way."

"Is that your arm?"

"I thought it was yours."

"Huh, I didn't know it could bend that way."

"Owww! It can't."

"Is that you, Sam?"

"No, it's Reggie Sanders. *Of course it's me!*"

"Don't yell. I didn't get us into this mess."

"Sure you did. You fell right on top of me."

"Ooomph. Those were my ribs. I assume that was your elbow."

"Sorry."

"But who fell in to begin with?"

"Yeah, but if you hadn't tried to reach down here—"

"Hey! I was just trying to save you some embarrassment."

"Who cares about embarrassment? I just want out of the stupid hole."

"And I was trying to help you. See what happens next time you fall into a hole."

"Ow! That's my armpit!"

"Yuk!"

Finally, when Pete was standing straight and the boys were untangled, Sam said, "Now, how are we going to get out of here? Let's be quiet for a minute and think."

Thirty seconds passed.

"Thought of anything yet?" Pete asked.

"Not yet."

A minute passed.

Sam asked, "How 'bout you? Anything?"

"Well . . . ," Pete started. "Not really."

"What? What is it?"

"It won't help us, Sam."

"Anything. What is it?"

"Well, this Bible verse popped into my head. Miss Whitehead used to say it a lot."

"OK, Pete, what is it?"

"Don't laugh."

"What is it?"

"Promise you won't laugh."

"I won't laugh. Now what is it?"

CHOICE⇒

Turn to page 12.

Willy tried to run, but stopped immediately. His ankle hurt so badly, he could hardly put weight on it. "Maybe I'd better see your aunt after all," he told Tina.

The other boys helped carry Willy into the apartment building. Tina phoned her aunt at the clinic.

"Put ice on it!" Tina called to the others from the phone. The others scurried to the kitchen. Jill got the ice from the freezer. Sam and Pete checked the drawers for towels or plastic bags.

"My aunt says they can see him right away—if we can get him there," Tina reported.

Just then the front door opened. It was Willy's older brother, Clarence, calling, "Yo, Will! Guess what I found out today!" He turned to see Willy leaning back on the easy chair, feet up, being cared for by his friends.

"I see they're finally giving you the respect you deserve," Clarence quipped. Then he saw the ice pack. "What happened?"

They told him about the football game, the injury, and the clinic. "Well, let's not waste time, folks. Everyone into the Batmobile!"

Clarence, whom the Ringers all called Zeke, was going to be a freshman at George Mason University, in Fairfax. He drove a long, low Chrysler. It was completely black, except for a few bits of chrome. He called it the

"Batmobile" because he thought it looked like Batman's car. (Willy thought it looked like a piece of junk from the sixties.) Zeke loved moments like this—when he, like the caped crusader, could save someone in need. He raced toward the clinic, taking shortcuts and rolling through a few stop signs. "Holy Highways, Batman!" yelled Sam. "You could get us all killed!"

"Never fear, young dweebs," Zeke intoned, as he pulled into the clinic parking lot. Zeke and Chris went into the doctor's office with Willy and Tina's aunt, the nurse. The others stayed in the waiting room and flipped through old magazines.

When he came out, Willy was wearing an Ace bandage on his ankle and carrying a fancy ice pack in one hand. With his other arm, he was leaning on a crutch. "He's going to be fine," Chris said. "He just twisted it. Nothing serious."

"I just have to ice it every so often," Willy added. "I could be all better in a day or two."

On the drive home, Zeke said, "I almost forgot what I was going to tell you. I was in the phys ed office at school today, and guess who's coming to GMU tomorrow. The Washington Redskins!"

"No!"

"They need a place to work out. I guess there were too many reporters at their other field or something, so they're coming here. It's a really hush-hush thing."

"They're probably working on secret plays and stuff," said Chris.

"Wouldn't it be awesome if we could go and watch?" said Willy.

"You can hardly walk, bro," snapped Zeke. "You're not going anywhere."

"I'll be better tomorrow!"

"The nurse said *maybe.*"

"It would be neat, though," said Chris.

Zeke shook his head. "They're going to have it locked up. Extra security."

"Yeah," said Willy. "But we know how to sneak in. Remember, Zeke? You showed me how."

"I don't know, children. You could get in trouble."

"So?" said Chris innocently. "We're just kids."

"Yeah," joked Sam, "we're *supposed* to get in trouble."

"Yeah and you're real good at it, too," Zeke agreed with a chuckle.

CHOICE

Turn to page 42.

Just then, Sam remembered how bad the day had been so far. "With my luck," he said, "I'd just get lost down here. I'd better stay right where I am."

The voice in the distance stopped. He tried to pretend the passage wasn't there. He sat and waited for Pete to arrive.

In about ten minutes, a familiar face was peering down at him. "Never fear," said Pete, "Mr. Wizard is here."

"What took you so long?"

"Well, I wasn't sure where to get a ladder or rope around here, so I ran home. And then I thought about my Tallmaker."

"Tallmaker?"

Suddenly Pete was dropping a small metal device down to Sam in the pit. "It was my science project last year," Pete explained. "You see, my little sister always asked me to get things in the cupboards because I'm so tall and she's so short. So I made this thing that could sort of make her tall. Tallmaker, get it?"

"Pete, why didn't you just bring a ladder?"

"But this is great, see? I never thought I'd get to use the Tallmaker in a life-or-death situation."

"What are you talking about?"

"It's simple, Sam. I hook up the battery pack, which

sends an electric current to a motor that cranks the gears that push a rod attached to the small platform—"

"What am I supposed to do with this?"

"Oh," said Pete. "Just step on it."

Sam placed the device on the floor of the pit and stepped on its small metal platform. Up above, Pete held a joystick that was connected to the device with a wire. Pete pushed the button, and the gears began turning.

"I don't feel anything," Sam cried. "I'm doomed!"

"Just wait a minute, Sam."

"I've *been* waiting for the last half hour while you were—hey, it's moving. I'm moving up."

The Tallmaker lifted Sam two feet higher in the pit, high enough for Pete to grab his arm and pull him out. Once he was out, Sam just lay back on the grass, enjoying the sunshine. Pete pulled the Tallmaker out of the pit with the joystick wire.

"You know," Sam sighed, "that's really brilliant, Pete. Does your little sister really use that?"

"No," Pete answered. "She usually climbs on a chair. But she doesn't ask for my help anymore."

"I wonder why."

Pete wanted to head back to the Freeze, but Sam insisted that they go to the church. So they crossed the Common—carefully—and walked up to the open church doors.

The church gleamed white in the afternoon sun. It had received a new coat of paint two weeks earlier, and that made it look almost new. Pete still felt that the old building was kind of creepy, but Sam felt good about being there. He really felt his day was going to take a turn for the better.

The inner doors were slightly ajar. The boys walked slowly, reverently, up to them. One door had a wooden carving of a lion, the other a lamb. Sam reached up to pet the lion. It was just something he had started to do every time he went inside. Pete put out his hand to stroke the lion's wooden mane.

"Don't do that," Sam whispered sharply. "It'll bite your hand off." Pete stopped with his hand in midair. This didn't make sense, but he petted the lamb instead. Sam was already walking into the sanctuary.

It was looking nicer all the time. During the summer the Ringers had been helping Mr. Whitehead fix up the church. When they started, it had been a disaster area. But now the pews were all in line, bolted to the floor—cleaned and polished.

"Wait!" Sam said. "Did you hear that?" There was a voice again. This was deeper than the one he had heard in the pit. It seemed to come from the front of the sanctuary, but the boys couldn't figure out what it was saying.

CHOICE

Turn to page 63.

124

The Ringer adventures continue.

Little did they know their adventures would start *before* they got to the Redskins game. With Mr. Whitehead's plans for Sonny and his family, it looks as if the Ringers have other adventures ahead of them, too.

Make sure you haven't missed any of the adventures in the Choice Adventures series, and look for others to follow. You'll get to know Chris, Willy, Jill, Jim, Tina, Sam, Pete, and many others. You may even decide to become a Ringer, too.

THE END

Randy Petersen is a free-lance writer living in New Jersey. He has written youth material for Chapel of the Air and is the author of the book *Giving to the Giver,* also by Tyndale.